MISSING IN THE ISLANDS

A Midwest Cozy Mystery - Book 9

BY

DIANNE HARMAN

Published by: Dianne Harman
www.dianneharman.com

Interior, cover design and website by
Vivek Rajan

ISBN: 9781688560208

CONTENTS

ACKNOWLEDGMENTS

To all of my readers who have made this series so popular, thank you for buying and borrowing my books, reading them, reviewing them, and sharing them with others.

To Vivek, Connie, and Imani, thank you. Without you, this book would never have seen the light of day.

And to Tom, for everything you do!

Win FREE Paperbacks every week!

Go to www.dianneharman.com/freepaperback.html and get your FREE copies of Dianne's books and favorite recipes immediately by signing up for her newsletter.

Once you've signed up for her newsletter you're eligible to win three paperbacks. One lucky winner is picked every week. Hurry before the offer ends!

PROLOGUE

Marion Molesey watched her children walk up to the front of the church with a lump in her throat. She fiddled with the tissue in her hand, which she'd already squeezed so much it was now a stringy mess.

She'd never expected this.

Neither had her four babies who now stood at the front of the church facing a crowd of friends and mourners. She looked up at them as they stood in front of the altar. Twenty-one-year-old Liam was holding his head high, but his trembling lower lip gave him away. Natasha, eighteen, openly wept, as did Logan, sixteen.

And the baby of the family at fourteen, Betsy, looked pale and shell-shocked, her face almost matching her white-blonde hair. She had an illness that so far was not diagnosed. It brought on random attacks of pain and tiredness, and since the news broke about her father dying, she'd regressed to a point where she often couldn't get out of bed all day. Somehow, she'd managed to hobble to the front of the church on crutches, but Marion knew that single physical act would wipe her out for the rest of the day.

"Our father was the best dad anyone could ask for," Liam said, his voice wavering. He looked down at the paper he had clutched in his hands, which was shaking like a leaf. "He was kind and caring and always supported us."

He ducked his head, his face screwed up, then lifted his chin and said, "Thanks, Dad, for all the good years." Then he stammered badly, just managing to choke out, "I'll never forget you."

It broke Marion's heart to watch this. Her children didn't deserve this. Why was life so utterly unfair? Thousands and thousands of people had been whitewater rafting before. Why did Richard have to be the one in 200,000 to die, or whatever the statistic was? Why Richard?

Of course, he hadn't been perfect. He liked to drink, too much a little more often than Marion would have preferred, but he hadn't been an alcoholic by any stretch. He wasn't a morning person and on occasions could snap a little too quickly, but so what?

He had dubious fashion sense and a penchant for wearing socks with cartoon characters on them that clashed insanely with his business suits, but that didn't stop clients from taking him seriously. His thriving business consulting practice was a testament to that.

He'd bought his family a beautiful home, a large six-bedroom mansion on the outskirts of Lindsay, Kansas, a small college town about a two hour drive from Kansas City. It was set back a ways from the street with a gate and had a beautiful front yard with trees, bushes, and a profusion of flowers.

Marion had never had to work outside the home, although she did do some dressmaking work from time to time. She'd made clothes for herself in her youth, and had continued to make special outfits for her children when they were young, things she couldn't find in the stores.

From time to time, people came to her to make outfits for their children, like a communion suit or a special dress for Christmas Day. She charged much less than she could have, because she did it for the pure pleasure of making the garment

Natasha and Logan made their short speeches in front of the assembled mourners, and the last one to speak was Betsy.

"I miss my daddy every single day," she said. "I don't know if I'll ever get over it. Daddy, I know you're in heaven, looking down on us. Protect us, Daddy. We love you so much…"

Marion couldn't stop the hot tears flowing silently down her cheeks, although she'd thought she was all cried out since Richard had been declared missing and presumed dead two months earlier.

Perhaps the hardest thing about it was that the authorities hadn't found his body. For the first month of his disappearance, Marion had found herself waking up with a desperate hope burning in her chest. *He'll be found, I know he will,* she'd thought.

It was all some terrible nightmare, she'd convinced herself, *and Richard would walk through the door any moment with a huge smile. He'd banged his head when he was whitewater rafting, but managed to get to the riverbank.*

Unfortunately, he'd forgotten who he was or where he came from, and he spent some time wandering from town to town, and staying in hotels, desperately trying to remember who he was and what his life had previously been.

But then, in a flash of inspiration that was seemingly sent from God, he remembered. It all dawned on him. He rushed away from where he was standing in line at a bakery in a strange town, hailed a cab, and grinned and laughed with glee all the way home, urging the driver to go, "Faster! Faster! I have to see my family!"

He'd burst in the front door, shaking his head in disbelief. He'd wrap Marion up in his arms, then the kids, and tell them all about the strangest thing that had ever happened to him in his life.

Except none of that happened. The front door stayed firmly shut. Marion jumped at every creak the house made, rushing to the hallway to see if it was Richard coming into the house. It never was.

The police finally closed the missing persons case and ruled that it was an accidental death, with no body ever having been recovered.

When that happened, reality finally crashed around Marion. No longer able to live the fantasy of him coming home, she was faced with the reality of here and now.

There would be no money coming in. Richard had no life insurance. Thankfully they'd paid off most of their mortgage over the years, so there were only seven more years left on the loan, but even those would be a stretch for her to pay. And what about food? Clothing? Car payments?

And even worse. What about health costs? Tests for Betsy's condition had run into the tens of thousands of dollars. They'd had to remove her from the family's health insurance policy, because if they kept her on, the premiums would skyrocket. They'd paid for her tests out of their own money, each time hoping the next one would wrap up the mystery of her illness and get her on the right track to successful treatment.

Marion looked at them as they made their way back from the front of the church, Logan helping Betsy down the steps leading from the altar, and she felt a physical ache in her chest. Literal heartbreak.

It continued through the car ride home where their friends and family members were gathering after the service. It continued there as well, and she had to hide in the kitchen on more than one occasion so she could compose herself.

It continued after everyone had left, when she was cleaning up.

It was then that she found a note tucked under a stack of dirty plates.

Look more carefully into what happened, it read. *Your husband is not dead.*

CHAPTER ONE

Kat Denham and her friends, Lennon and Mitzi, met in the parking lot of the Lindsay Tennis Club.

It was a very rare occurrence when Lennon managed to get any spare time, given she homeschooled six kids while also maintaining an immaculately maintained home, a burgeoning blog, and was a preacher at a megachurch.

Kat knew it was a huge deal for her to find time to meet with Mitzi and Kat, and Kat truly appreciated it. Lennon's in-laws were looking after the kids for the morning, and she turned up in a sleek workout ensemble, her blonde hair pulled back in an immaculate ponytail.

Mitzi was an acupuncture doctor and operated a large clinic devoted to that form of holistic treatment. Thankfully, due to the success of her clinic, she could choose her own hours, so she'd had no problem making time to join Kat and Lennon at the tennis club.

"Mitzi, this is my friend, Lennon Forbes. We met when she organized a writers' convention where I was a speaker. Lennon, this is Dr. Mitzi Brown, acupuncturist extraordinaire. She owns the huge acupuncture clinic we have here in town."

"Pleased to meet you," Lennon said, smiling warmly and putting out her hand.

Mitzi shook it with a kind look on her face. "If you're a friend of Kat's, you're a friend of mine."

"Thanks, and vice versa," Lennon said. They walked through the gate into the tennis club, past the numerous courts and toward the clubhouse, where the women's tennis group was due to meet before they started playing tennis.

"Now, Kat, I'm going to try my best, but I must warn you, I'm real rusty," Lennon said.

"Me, too," Mitzi said. "Literally." She unzipped her tennis racquet case and showed them a little rust spot on her racquet. She rolled her eyes. "I didn't realize that was there until I was about to get in the car. I'll have to get a new one."

"That is, if you like playing," Kat said.

"I used to," Mitzi said. "It's been a long time since I've done anything athletic. I have a cross trainer at home, and Rex and I often go for walks, but that's all."

Kat smiled. "Same here. I take my two dogs, Jazz and Rudy, on walks almost every day, but I decided I needed something to get the heart pumping a little more."

Lennon nodded. "I agree. I mean, running around after the little ones at home keeps me active, but you're right, Kat. What's lacking is the cardio."

They were silent for a moment. Mitzi bent down and let some trailing flowers at the side of the path run through her fingers. "They've landscaped this place beautifully, haven't they?"

"Yes, they really have" Lennon responded.

It truly was gorgeous, with arches over the walkway where trailing flowers danced down in whites and pale blues, and neatly trimmed bushes surrounded the edge of the tennis club. Tall mature trees were set further back, giving the impression they were immersed in nature.

The landscaping around the clubhouse was spectacular as well, with antique-looking steps and patios at three different levels, interspersed with beds planted with flowers and fragrant bushes. The clubhouse itself was wide and white with a porch running the entire length of it.

"It is beautiful," Kat said. "And that's a compliment coming from you, Mitzi. Lennon, she's an avid gardener. Honestly, her yard is a little slice of paradise."

"I'd love to see it sometime," Lennon said. "I need some inspiration for ours. I have to admit that it's getting a little neglected. We pretty much just mow the grass, and my husband and older kids trim the bushes every now and then. It's neat and tidy, but it's a little lackluster."

"Anytime," Mitzi said. "And if it wouldn't be too presumptuous of me, I'd be happy to come to your house and give you some ideas and even do some little sketches for you. I enjoy doing that sort of thing."

"Oh, that would be great," Lennon said.

Mitzi smiled. "My pleasure."

"At the least, I'd have to repay you with a home-cooked meal," Lennon said.

"Mitzie, snap up that offer," Kat said. "Lennon's a wonderful cook. And one of her sons, Gideon, is a fantastic baker. I think once you've eaten there, you'll never want to leave."

Mitzi grinned. "Then, in that case, consider it done!"

When they reached the clubhouse, they went inside. It was

somewhat old-fashioned, but clean and bright, with a bar, a kitchen, and doors leading off to dressing rooms and bathrooms.

There were only three other women there. Two were older, perhaps in their 70s, looking fit with sleekly-styled short haircuts, and a woman who looked to be in her mid-50s. The two older women were talking animatedly, banging their tennis racquets against their pristine white sneakers, while the other woman sat alone, hunched over.

She seemed to have no confidence whatsoever. Her hair limply straggled down past her shoulders, looking like rats' tails running over her white tennis outfit, and she didn't make eye contact with Kat, Lennon, or Mitzi when they walked in.

"Glenys," Mitzi exclaimed, walking over to one of the older women.

"Ah, Dr. Brown," Glenys said. "You really must go to Dr. Brown's acupuncture clinic, Susie. She's worked absolute miracles on my shoulder." Susie didn't look convinced, so Glenys continued, "Acupuncture helps with pretty much anything, you know. Arthritis, weight loss, backpain, practically anything you can think of.

"I didn't know much about it, but they have lots of informative leaflets in the clinic. In fact, I'll pick one up for you the next time I'm there."

"All right," Susie said. "Now, let me organize the lunches." She clapped her hands together to get everyone's attention, although she really didn't need to, since there were only a few of them there, and no one else was talking.

"Hello, everyone. Welcome to the women's weekly tennis group. It's good to see both the familiar and the new faces. For those of you who haven't been here before, we play a couple of hours of tennis, both singles and doubles, circling through different pairings. Then we come back here and have a sandwich and salad lunch. The choice today is chicken salad or egg salad. Please let me know which one you'd like, and I'll take the orders into the kitchen."

When that was done, they went outside and onto the tennis courts. The sad-looking woman tied her hair up in a messy bun. Kat saw the dark rings under her eyes and her tiny slivers of fingernails, which had obviously been bitten down. Kat wondered what was going on in her life to make her look so unhappy.

Susie clapped her hands once they were outside. "Okay, everyone, first we'll have a quick warm up. I apologize if I get any of your names wrong, since I've never been very good with them. So, Mimi…"

"Mitzi," Mitzi said with a smile.

Susie clapped her hand to her forehead. "Mitzi. Mitzi, Mitzi, Mitzi. Okay, Mitzi, you'll go with Glenys. Lennon, we'll play together. And Kat… it is, Kat, isn't it?"

"Yep," Kat said with a smile.

Susie nodded. "You'll go with Marion. And then we'll regroup after ten minutes or so and start playing some sets." She dug into a large sports bag sitting on the ground next to her feet and said, "Here are some balls, ladies. Let's get playing!"

So, the depressed looking lady was called Marion. Kat smiled at her, as they walked to a far court together.

"I probably need to warn you," Kat said. "I'm going to be a little rusty. Do you play often?"

Marion looked away. She smiled, but her eyes didn't light up. "I come every week."

"Oh, great," Kat said. "Well, at least great for you. You'll probably thrash me. I just hope you'll be patient with me."

Marion simply nodded, but Kat didn't get the impression she was

9

being standoffish or deliberately rude. It seemed like her mind was so full of worrying, she didn't have any space left to register anything else.

As it turned out, Marion was fantastic at tennis. Kat could tell Marion was going easy on her by the way she looked so confident on the court. It was as if the mousy, preoccupied woman was gone, and a top-flight competitor had taken her place. She held her head high. She moved with grace, and she didn't miss a single shot.

Kat surprised herself, though, by how decent she was. It had been a really long time since she'd played tennis, but after a few balls that went into the net, or outside the lines on Marion's side, she got a feel for the racquet and was soon in the swing of things.

Marion recognized this, and took it up a notch, until Kat was diving all over the court, stretching for ambitious backhands and beginning to work up a sweat.

"Nice shot!" Marion said, beaming when Kat returned an aggressive volley.

Kat looked up and smiled at her. "Thanks!" she said,

They cycled through partners for the next couple of hours. Mitzi and Kat were well-matched. Lennon turned out to be terrible, which was a bit of a shock, because she was usually good at everything, with a wonderful husband, immaculate household, amazingly-behaved and pristinely dressed brood of six homeschooled kids, a fledgling writing career, a flair for baking, a talent for organizing, and... well, the list was as long as Kat's arm.

But she was a good sport about it. She was red in the face and puffing. "Now, this is a great workout," she said. "What fun! I do apologize, Glenys. I'm so lousy this must be really boring for you."

"Nonsense," Glenys said, picking up a ball that was next to the net. "Everyone has to start somewhere." Then she went back to the service line and bounced the ball expertly next to her white sneaker.

She then made a slow and easy serve.

Lennon managed to hit it with the frame of the racquet, and it made a wild bounce over her head and out of the court. Lennon sighed, then laughed at herself. "Looks like I'm starting from a little kid level."

When they'd finished playing, they went inside for their lunch of sandwiches and salad. There was a huge pitcher of iced tea, which was quickly consumed.

Mitzi and Lennon were chatting away with Glenys and Susie, the tennis having loosened them all up socially. Kat sat next to Marion, who looked flushed and happy. It was quiet a transformation from the way she'd looked when they'd first started.

"You're a great player," Kat said.

"Thanks," Marion said, looking a little embarrassed. "I think tennis is the only thing that keeps me sane sometimes."

Kat nodded. "I feel the same about walking my dogs."

"That would be no good for me," Marion said. "Still too much time to think. That's what I like about tennis. You have to concentrate on the next shot. There's no thinking about anything else, or you'll miss the ball."

"I agree. You have to stay sharp to play this game," Kat said as she took a bite of her chicken salad sandwich.

"Yes," Marion said with a laugh. "With the amount I've got going on in my life, I've started to come twice a week. If things continue as they are, I might just end up a tennis champion."

Kat got the feeling Marion wanted to confide in her. "It sounds like things are sort of tough for you right now."

"Yes, they are. You see my husband died recently."

"Oh, dear," Kat said, feeling a tug on her heart for two reasons. First, she imagined how she'd feel if Blaine Evans, her District Attorney husband who she'd married just a few years ago, was to die. And second, because she'd been through it herself with her first husband Greg, who was father to her grown up daughter Lacie.

"I'm remarried now, but I'm also a widow. My former husband died in a car accident."

Marion reached out, took her hand, and squeezed it. "Mine in a whitewater rafting accident."

"Oh no. I'm so sorry."

Marion went back to eating her sandwich. She shook her head. "It's the kids I'm worried about. I have four children, two sons and two daughters. Especially my youngest, Betsy. She's not very well physically, and she and my husband were so close, and…" She swallowed hard. "Well, never mind."

Kat was about to say something comforting when Glenys leaned over the table, her eyes shining. "It was you!" she said. "I never knew."

Kat laughed nervously. "What was me?"

"Mitzi here was telling me that it was you who solved the murder of Chance Nelson, the newspaper owner, and Ashlee Nelson's husband!"

Kat paused. "Guilty," she said. She really didn't like it when people made a fuss about it.

"Not only that," Lennon said. "When a writer was killed at my book launch, she helped figure out who did that as well. You see, Kat writes murder mystery books, so she's got the right kind of investigative mind." Lennon beamed at her proudly.

Kat smiled. "This lady is far too kind."

Thankfully, they were nearly done with their sandwiches, since Kat really didn't want to have to go into a long explanation about her murder investigations, which looked like it would be happening if she stayed there much longer.

"Well, I've got to go home and feed my dogs," Kat said. "This was absolutely wonderful. I'll definitely be coming again next week. See you all."

"Goodbye, Kat!" they all said.

When Kat looked at Marion, Marion's look was full of intensity. It was as if she wanted to say something, but couldn't. Kat wondered what it was as she made her way back to her car in the parking lot.

CHAPTER TWO

The next morning, Kat woke up early. The sun had begun to rise and the room was gradually lifting out of daybreak into the day. Blaine was still asleep as she snuggled into his back and held him for a while.

She was so thankful to have him in her life. Truthfully, she'd never thought she'd find love again and certainly she wasn't looking for it. For the first couple of years after Greg's death, she couldn't even think about it. She was personally grief-stricken, but also heartbroken for Lacie, who had only been eleven at the time of her father's death. The two of them clung together emotionally and often talked about "Daddy." They reminisced fondly about him almost every day.

But as time passed, Greg's death really sank in. He wasn't going to be coming back. Life had to move on. That said, Kat had been in no rush to date. She'd met Blaine Evans just after he'd become the District Attorney. His lopsided smile that crinkled his kind eyes and his gentle, calm manner won her over. Thankfully, Lacie quickly became a fan of his as well, and not long after, Kat and Blaine had married.

In fact, Lacie now considered him so much a part of the family that he was "Grandpa" to Lacie's baby girl, Florence, who was now one year old and staggering about giggling, toddling on her feet, and amazed at everything she came in contact with.

Lacie was scheduled to return to work at the child psychologists' office where she was training in a week, after she'd taken a long maternity leave. She and Kat had arranged to squeeze in as many daytime outings as they could that final week, to make the most of the last days of her maternity leave.

They'd agreed that Kat would look after Florence two days a week, she'd go to daycare two days, and Lacie would have her for the final day of the work week, since she was working condensed hours over four days.

So Lacie and Kat had a few little outings planned. On the agenda was a trip with Florence to the petting zoo, get massages and facials and then have lunch while Blaine babysat Florence for the morning, take Florence to the play center, and finally, take a long walk around the park with the dogs. Kat was very much looking forward to all of it.

"Kat?" Blaine said softly.

"Oh, you're awake, honey." She snuggled into his neck and kissed him on the back of his head.

"Just about," he said. "You sound remarkably lively for this early in the morning."

"Well, I've been awake for a little while now."

"Something on your mind, darling?"

"No. Only how much I love you."

Blaine chuckled. "Sounds like you've been writing romance novels lately."

"Nope," Kat said. "But thanks to you, I've been living one."

Blaine turned around and looked at her with his laughing eyes. "You're saying all the right things this morning."

She grinned. "It's not just steamy romps I write about under my Sexy Cissy pen name, you know. Sometimes my characters are actually in love."

"Like us," he said, intertwining his fingers with hers.

"Like us," she nodded.

"Though we're far too dull to write about," he said with a grin. "I'm not a billionaire sheikh."

"Speak for yourself," Kat said, "because I'm fascinating."

"Yes, you are. Far too fascinating, sometimes, with your love of investigating all these dangerous situations which just seem to come to you from out of nowhere," he said. "You're going to give me a heart attack over them one of these days."

"Well, it's not as if I plan on them coming along, do I?" Kat asked. "I'm not lurking in the bushes with a magnifying glass in my hand waiting for someone to drop dead." She was starting to feel a little indignant. This was the one sore spot in their otherwise perfect relationship, and she didn't feel like talking about it.

She sat up in the bed. "Anyway, what do you want for breakfast? I know you have a busy day today with the police chief."

Blaine sighed. His eyes searched her face for a moment. He looked like he wanted to say something, but then thought better of it. Eventually he said, "Kat, you know I am very proud of what you've done."

She broke into a smile. "As well you should be, mister," she said, batting him with a pillow. "And it's not like your job's the safest, either, as we well know." Not too long ago there had been a threat against Blaine's life.

He put his arms out and after a moment of playful resistance, she allowed him to hug her. "Eggs," he whispered into her ear.

Kat burst out laughing. "That's your version of sweet nothings, honey?"

He chuckled. "I'm sorry. I'm just not Sexy Cissy hero material, am I?"

"Well, perhaps you could work on the sweet talk," she said, getting up and putting on her robe. "Now, I'm going to go make you those eggs you so sweetly cooed about."

After a leisurely breakfast, Kat drove over to Lacie's home to pick Florence and her up. Florence was at an adorable age, just starting to talk, and as soon as Kat walked in the door, she said, "Gamma!" which was her gummy version of Grandma, burst into a huge smile, and ran over to Kat on unsteady feet. Kat scooped her up and tickled Florence until she squealed. "Who's going to the park?" she said. "Who's going to the park?"

"Park!" Florence chirped.

They took off with Jazz and Rudy in the back of the car, Florence strapped tightly into her car seat, clutching her little teddy bear she carried everywhere with her. Lacie sat next to Kat in the front seat.

"Are you looking forward to going back to work?" Kat asked.

"Hmm… that's a tough one. I mean, I'll be glad to be studying again. You know, being one step closer to becoming a qualified child psychologist," Lacie said. "But at the same time, I'm consumed with mom guilt. I'm barely ever away from Florence, and now, well, I'll only be with her three days a week."

Kat sighed. "That's got to be hard on you."

"Yes, it is," Lacie said as she chewed her lower lip. "Tyler told me I could be a stay-at-home mom if I wanted to. Money would be tight for a while, since he's not fully qualified as a veterinarian yet and won't be for a couple of years, but we could scrape by."

"That's definitely an option. What do you think you're going to do?"

"The thing is, I want to go back to work," Lacie said. "I absolutely love being a mother, but I also want my career."

Kat nodded. "There's nothing wrong with that."

"Are you sure? I feel so guilty."

"Don't," Kat said. "You're a wonderful, kind, loving mother and Florence will always know that. She's not going to feel neglected or left behind, trust me. She'll be having a wonderful time at daycare with the other little kids, and you know I'm going to spoil her rotten the two days I have her." Kat reached over and squeezed Lacie's hand. "Don't worry about it. It's going to be fine."

"Okay," Lacie said, her voice a little wobbly and sounding as if she wasn't quite convinced.

"It's also normal to be emotional and guilty about it," Kat said. "I was a stay-at-home mom when I had you, but many of my friends worked, and all of them, without exception, said the first day they left their child at daycare they cried as soon as they got back in the car."

"Oh, I know I'll be one of those," Lacie said. "You know me, Mom. Since I got pregnant, I'll cry at a health insurance commercial."

Kat chuckled. "Tyler informs me if there's a Lifetime movie on you have to leave the room, or risk an inundation."

Lacie shook her head at herself and laughed. "Sad, but true, Mom."

When they arrived at the park, Florence was sound asleep in her car seat. Lacie carefully took her out of it and put her in her stroller. She flopped back in the cutest way, her little mouth slightly open. Kat stroked her caramel-colored curls. "Awww," she said, filled with love and gratitude for her little granddaughter.

Jazz and Rudy both peered in the stroller as well. Thankfully they were well-trained dogs with very caring natures, and Kat felt they were quite protective of little Florence.

They took a long stroll through the park. It was cool for a June day, with a pleasant temperature and a nice refreshing breeze which made the leaves rustle in the trees overhead.

When they were deep in the park, Florence woke up, so they went over to the play area. Florence strained to be let out of the stroller, an excited look on her face. As soon as Lacie took her out of her stroller, Florence charged her way over to the sandpit. Kat and Lacie shared a smile.

When Lacie went over to supervise Florence, Kat's phone rang. She didn't recognize the number, but it was local. "Kat Denham," she answered.

"Hello, Kat. It's Marion. Marion Molesey."

"Oh, hello, Marion," Kat said, desperately racking her brain to remember where she knew her from. Then she remembered - the tennis club.

"I'm really sorry to bother you." She sounded as if she had reverted to the mousy, apologetic person she'd been when she wasn't smashing the ball on the tennis court.

"Not at all," Kat said kindly.

"I wanted to tell you something," Marion said. "But it's only really suitable if I do it in person."

"Oh, okay… Well, would you like to come over to my home tonight? I'm out with my daughter and granddaughter for the day, but I'll be home this evening. Perhaps for dinner?"

"Yes, if it's not too much trouble."

"Oh, no," Kat said. "I'd be delighted. Why don't you plan on coming to my home at 7:00? Here's my address." She recited it to Marion who wrote it down.

*****

Later that evening, Kat was at home, cooking a dinner of sausage plait, or more commonly called a picnic pie, new potatoes, and steamed broccoli. Kat liked to be adventurous when it came to cooking, trying dinner recipes from all over the world.

Sausage plait was one she'd tried a couple of times and liked to serve in summer when she wanted something delicious and a little impressive, but not too complicated. All she had to do was season some sausage rolls, wrap them in a puff pastry sheet and cut them into bite size pieces. Then they went in the oven for forty minutes. Simple!

While she was cooking dinner, she wondered what Marion was going to tell her. She remembered just how preoccupied she'd looked before she'd begun to play tennis, and how her nails were bitten down to tiny slivers.

Kat also remembered their conversation about their late husbands. Perhaps it had something to do with that? Whatever it was, she felt it would be something confidential and slightly sensitive.

It worked out quite well in that Blaine had to work late. At the moment his caseload was high, and he and the police chief had more to get through than they bargained for, so she and Marion would have some privacy. Then when Blaine got home, Marion would be gone and she could focus her attention on him. It had turned out to be a win-win situation.

Once the sausage plait had been made, she cooked some sausage meat on the stove and put it in Jazz and Rudy's food bowls. They wolfed it down gratefully.

Kat put the sausage rolls in the oven and then she worked on writing at the kitchen table, the dogs ambling lazily over to her feet once they'd had their fill. Kat often had a game she played with herself while something was in the oven. How many words could she crank out during this time? Once she'd managed one thousand words in half an hour, but she had yet to replicate that. Five hundred words an hour was more normal for her.

As usual when she was writing, time flew by, and before she knew it, the oven was beeping. She'd timed it perfectly, too, because before she'd even had the chance to get it out of the oven, there was a knock at the door.

"Marion," Kat said as she opened the door. "It's good to see you."

Marion looked as unconfident as ever. "Hi, Kat," she said quietly, trying to smile, but not looking at all happy.

"Come in, come in," Kat said, unperturbed. "I'm just taking a sausage plait out of the oven. We'll be having it for dinner. It's an English dish."

"Oh, right."

Definitely not chatty, Kat thought.

Jazz and Rudy weren't the types of dogs who rushed at the door when someone knocked on it, but they did make their way into the hallway to see who'd arrived, and then followed Kat and Marion back into the kitchen. Marion eyed them warily.

Kat noticed and said, "They don't bite or anything like that, Marion, honestly. They're very kind, gentle dogs."

Marion nodded. She looked like she was a million miles away.

Kat took the sausage plait out of the oven. "The potatoes and broccoli are ready, but we'll have to wait a few minutes for these to cool."

"It's fine."

"Would you like a drink while we're waiting for it to cool?" Kat asked.

"No, thank you."

"Okay. Shall we sit down?"

"Sure."

Kat sat at the far side of the kitchen table, gesturing for Marion to sit down opposite her. She did so, and started to bite her nails, except there were barely any there, so she was gnawing the tips of her fingers. Her eyes stayed on the table surface.

"Marion, you look really distressed."

"Look at this." Marion dug into her pocket, pulled out a scrap of paper, and pushed it across the table towards Kat as if she didn't want to touch it herself.

Kat read it. *Look more carefully into what happened,* it said. *Your husband is not dead.* She frowned, confused, and looked up at Marion quizzically. "I don't, I don't understand what this is about."

"They never found my husband's body," Marion choked out.

"Oh…" Kat said, as it dawned on her.

"I think they're saying he faked his own death," Marion said. "I found it after people had come to our house following the church service. It was beneath some dirty plates."

Kat sighed and shook her head. "No wonder you're distressed, Marion. This is a lot to deal with."

"I've been torturing myself with it," she said. "The two scenarios cast such different stories on my life. Either I was married to a kind man who tragically died. Or I was married to a heartless liar, who would abandon his children, even his sick child, and cause them to be grief-stricken. And I don't know which one it is. I look at pictures of Richard, and I don't know whether to love him or hate him."

Kat sighed. "Yes, I can see where you would wonder."

"Look at this," Marion said. She took her smartphone from her pocket and played a video for Kat. It was the whole family having an outing at the local bowling alley, with Marion and her husband horsing around, singing little snippets of songs, dancing, and looking very much in love. "That was just six months ago."

"You look so happy," Kat said. In that video, Marion looked ten years younger. Her eyes were all lit up with love and happiness. It was heartbreaking to watch, because of the comparison between then and now.

"I was," Marion said bitterly. She looked down, gulped, then looked back up again, clearly trying to force herself to look confident. "I expect you know why I'm here then, Kat, don't you?"

Kat nodded. "You want me to investigate. To find out if he's alive, and if so, where he is."

Marion looked desperate. "Would you? I mean, you don't have to, of course, it's just, well, I heard them saying how great you were at investigating, and…"

"I'll do it," Kat said. "When I talked to you at tennis the other day, and you mentioned your husband had died, it brought back all the feelings and things I'd experienced when my husband unexpectedly died.

"No one should have to wonder whether or not their husband is alive or dead, particularly when children are involved. You deserve to know the truth, as do your children. Yes, I'll see what I can do. If I'd been in your situation, I'd hope that someone would have helped me."

Marion smiled. It changed her whole face. "Thank you so much. What can I do for you in return? I wish I could pay you a whole load of money, but..."

"No, no, no," Kat said, wagging her finger. "No money, but there is something you can do for me in return."

"What's that?"

Kat smiled. "Teach me how to play tennis like you do."

Marion smiled back. "That's a deal."

CHAPTER THREE

Latimer Keir quickly stepped out of his chauffeur-driven limousine and strode towards the polished skyscraper in front of him, his coattails flying out behind him. He was tall and commanding in everything he did. He wasn't particularly handsome, but women still fell all over themselves attempting to become acquainted with him. He oozed power from every pore in his body.

In the business world, this was a great asset for Latimer Keir and he used it to the maximum. People, men and women alike, lost their footing when they talked to him. Even the most confident businesspeople wilted in his presence. He steamrolled over people with business deals heavily weighted in his favor.

Unfortunately for Keir, though, there were people in the world like Richard Molesey. Keir had underestimated him, and it had been a grave mistake.

A bumbling, small-town pretender, Keir had written in his secret black book of contacts. It was full of scathing insults on people's characters, of course. He enjoyed nothing more than studying people and finding their weak spots. And then, using those weaknesses against them for his own benefit. Whatever he won, pride, the business deal, the girl, it was worth it. Keir was always the biggest man in the room. He had to be.

Richard Molesey was from Kansas, for goodness sake. "How much more country bumpkin could he be?" Keir had laughed with his only friend and business partner, Dustin Kowalski. Their office was based in Houston, Texas.

Kowalski, though slightly less mercenary than Keir, also wanted Richard out of the picture, so that Keir & Kowalski, their commercial real estate firm, could cut a deal that would make them a huge profit. They wanted to buy a large old tract of land with an abandoned warehouse on it. Evidently Molesey didn't know the value of it.

He wasn't the owner, but was selling it on behalf of a client of his, Newmans, and taking a cut. This was a client they were hoping to take advantage of over the next few years, since it was a large landowner in Kansas, and Keir & Kowalski saw potential in the state.

They planned to tear down the warehouse, put in roads and utilities, and then sell it off to businesses as an out of town retail park. It was just outside a reasonably sized city, which was expanding, and there was certainly a need for such a place. They'd make a killing.

They'd tried to play it down to Richard Molesey. They'd said the land was practically worthless, however their accountant had urged them to buy something before the tax year was out, and this, sure enough, was something. Even if it was only marginally better than nothing.

Richard had agreed to sell it for just 65% of the asking price, because it was going to be a quick all cash sale, but at the last minute he'd pulled out and wanted a higher offer. That made Keir angry. But Richard had done something worse. Much worse. And Keir had just found out about it.

That morning, after arriving at the offices of Keir and Kowalski, Keir didn't greet one person who said hello to him. He was on the warpath, and his eyes were like a blazing fire, burning through anything he looked at. When he got to the penthouse floor where he and his partner had their offices, his assistant took one look at him and scurried back to her desk, burying herself in paperwork.

He violently threw open the door to Kowalski's office. "Dustin," he said tersely. If he'd been the kind of man to yell, he would have been screaming and cursing, but Keir had spent his life perfecting a cool, calm exterior. He was as smooth as a snake.

"What?" Kowalski asked as he looked up from his desk, where he was typing on his computer.

"Switch off all of your electronic devices immediately," Keir said. "Phones, computers, everything."

Keir was never asked to explain himself, not even by Kowalski. With others, it was because they feared him too much to disobey. With Kowalski, it was a mix of that fear, but also implicit trust.

Their relationship was a strange one. They respected each other, even loved each other, in a sense. But they also knew they were both as evil as the other, Keir in a scheming, deliberate way, and Kowalski in an ambitious, utilitarian way.

They each knew that if the opportunity came for an advancement for either of them, which required throwing the other under the bus, they'd jump at the chance with no regrets. But it hadn't happened, yet. For the time being they enjoyed throwing other people under the bus, together.

Kowalski turned off all his devices, including his phone. Keir was too amped up to sit down, but he finally did, forcing himself to do so. He never wanted to betray strong emotions, even in the worst of situations.

"What's going on?" Kowalski asked.

"It's that guy, Molesey."

Kowalski smirked. "What about him?"

"Somehow he's gotten hold of one of our private conversations," Keir said. "It's the one where we discuss the scale of the deal, how much it would benefit our firm, and how much they were losing out."

All the color drained from Kowalski's face. "How did he get it? We didn't discuss that in writing."

"He has a voice recording," Keir said. "I got a call from him. If we don't transfer two million dollars into his personal account, he's going to leak it to every firm in Kansas and make sure we're shut out of the market. Our entire business plan for the next five years will be ruined. All that networking and getting our foot in the door will have been for nothing."

Kowalski leaned back in his chair. He took a flask from his desk drawer and took a long drink. "What do you think we should do?"

"Our options are as follows. One, we can pay the money. But in that case, he still holds power over us, because he'd still have the recording. Even if he said he'd destroyed it, that's no guarantee he doesn't have it backed up. He could come back at us the next day, and the day after that, requesting millions more until he ruins our business."

"You're right," Kowalski said.

"We could go to the authorities and have him arrested for blackmail. What we did was not illegal."

"Of course not. We'd never do anything illegal."

That part was true. They were deeply immoral, but never, ever illegal. It wasn't worth the hassle, they'd reasoned.

"Or we could kill him," Keir continued, "and break our pattern of legality."

Kowalski crinkled his nose in disdain. "That's a little… messy, Keir."

"It doesn't have to be."

"Our other option is to brave it out," Kowalski said. "Surely all the businesses in Kansas can't be do-gooders who care about locker room talk. If they're cutting a deal with proper legal advice, they may not even care."

"Damage control. That's what's needed in this situation," Keir said, leaning his elbows on the table and placing his hands in a triangle under his chin. "Somehow, it feels like we'd be retreating if we did anything less than kill him."

Which they never, ever did.

"How did he even get the recording?" Kowalski asked. "If he had the means to do that, what else does he have the means to do?"

"We'll need to change all our telephone lines and all of our electronics," Keir said. "We need to immediately install some kind of blockers on these things. Get the nerdiest of the tech nerds to handle it."

"Yes, I agree. We've got to do it immediately."

They sank into silence, both deep in thought.

Keir stared out the glass windows that ran from floor to ceiling and provided a spectacular view of Houston, and then said, "I think we should take him out."

Kowalski was looking more stressed by the minute. "I didn't get into this business to commit murder."

"You wouldn't be committing murder," Keir said. "Someone would do it on your behalf."

"No," Kowalski said. "The more people that are involved, the bigger the potential for leaks. If he has a recording, he may have tapped into all our lines. How will we arrange this? He could have advanced technology tracking us."

"Why would he do that?"

"For fun, I don't know. He's an unknown quantity. We thought he was a clueless country bumpkin and now we've learned he's something altogether different from that."

Being wrong was physically painful for Keir. A strong searing pain lanced through his chest. "He definitely got the better of us."

Kowalski took another swig from his flask and said, "Keir. I think we'll have to do this ourselves. Cleanly. With no chance of being caught. No one else should know a word about it, not even a breath. We'll plan it meticulously, and we will get away with it, then continue our business campaign in Kansas."

Keir nodded slowly. "Kowalski, you're a marvel."

"No," Kowalski said. "I'm just infinitely practical."

CHAPTER FOUR

Frederick James couldn't believe it. Helen was gone. Well, anyway she wasn't in her bed where she should have been after getting off work from her late night job as a bartender. He looked at her bed again, even turning over the bedsheets. Nothing. He turned over the bedsheets again. He went on a rampage through the apartment looking everywhere for her. Again, nothing.

His daughter and son, both toddlers in diapers, were screaming, tears pouring down their cheeks, but he was in too much of a panic to comfort them.

Where was Helen?

Where was she?

It was like she'd disappeared into thin air.

But then, when he went into the kitchen, he saw the notes.

A pile of notes. Stacked on the counter.

His heart dropped as he touched them. The children had followed him in, and were tugging at his pajama bottoms. He spread the three notes out on the counter. One said Frederick. One said Emersyn, the name of their daughter. One said Garrick, the name of their son.

He didn't want to open them. He felt his heart might burst open and he'd drop to the floor, dead.

But he was compelled to.

He opened the one with his own name on it, unfolding the paper.

I'm so sorry, Freddie, it read. *I had to. I had to get out. You'll never see me again. I'm so sorry. Look after the kids. You'll all be better off without me.*

That was all.

That was all.

That was all?

He went back into the living room, the kids trailing behind him. He just managed to get to the couch before his legs buckled and he dropped onto it. He couldn't cry. He couldn't scream. He couldn't even think. He just sat there, totally numb.

The kids climbed up on him, crawling all over him, tugging at his cheeks and at his hair. He just sat there. The pain as Emersyn pulled his hair hard barely even registered.

He wasn't sure how long he sat there. But at some point, a huge surge of energy overtook him, and he got to his feet. He bent over and hugged his children. "Okay, my loves. It's time to get you to daycare." Although his heart was breaking in his chest, he knew what he had to do.

He went through all the motions of their usual morning routine. Helen worked nights at a bar, so she was never up in the morning. He'd done the routine so many times he could do it with his eyes closed. He smiled, sang snippets of silly songs, and made getting their clothes on into a game. The entire time he was disconnected, his mind racing, making a plan for what he was going to do next.

By the time he'd gotten the kids to daycare, they'd clearly

forgotten all about his frantic mad rush around the apartment that morning, and settled into their usual routine. To them, it was just another normal day.

As soon as he left them at daycare, he took the notes for the kids out of his pocket. He hadn't read them yet. They both said the same thing. *Mommy loves you and she's very sorry.* Nothing more than that.

When he'd finishing reading them, he called his brother, Samuel. "Helen's gone," he told him. "She left notes. I'm not sure if she's looking to kill herself or leaving or what. The notes weren't clear. I'm going to go out and look for her. Could you help me?"

"Be there in a few," Samuel said. "I'm just on the way to work. I'll call them, and come meet you. Where are you?"

"I'll meet you by the Brooklyn Bridge. That's the first place I'm going, just in case."

"Have you called the cops?"

"No," Frederick said. "I don't think there's enough to go on at this point. I just want to see if I can find her."

"Your call," Samuel said. "See you as soon as I can."

"Thanks." Frederick hung up the phone and headed to the Brooklyn Bridge. The traffic was gridlocked at that time of day, so he knew it'd be much quicker to just walk there.

What started as a fast-paced walk turned into a jog, and then that turned into a sprint, as he tried to weave in and out of pedestrians on the sidewalk, sometimes not always managing it. "Sorry! Sorry!" he said, when he bumped into people by accident.

When he got to the Brooklyn Bridge, he surveyed the entire length of it, but he couldn't make out any figures standing at the edge ready to jump. Now wasn't the best time of day for a suicide attempt anyway. There would be too much attention.

Maybe she'd already done it.

Maybe it wasn't suicide at all.

He didn't know what to think about anything. His brain was fast turning to mush.

Regardless, he still ran the length of Brooklyn Bridge, desperately looking into each and every face, hoping he might see Helen staring back at him.

He knew they'd been going through a rocky patch in their marriage. Well, in truth, it had been rocky since Emersyn was born three years earlier. Helen had gotten pregnant with Garrick three months after Emersyn's birth, when there was still a glimmer of hope left for their relationship. After he was born, there was none.

They fought constantly. They rarely made love and only if she was drunk. Actually, that was quite often, since she drank on the job, but most of the time her inebriation caused her to lash out at him and call him disgusting names, rather than becoming amorous.

But now, with his heart in his throat, all Frederick could remember was the good times. The heady rush of falling in love with her. The tender moments they'd shared over the years. There had even been some more recent moments, when they'd watched TV together with his arm around her.

She'd cuddled into his chest, and he'd stroked her hair. There had been times when they both went into the kids' room, and watched them as they slept, sharing a secret smile about how adorable they were.

Those kinds of moments made Frederick believe maybe they could be a happy family one day. Maybe it was just a tough time, having two young children in diapers. He'd heard those years weren't easy. He'd thought in a few years they'd come out on the other side and laugh about it. They'd hold hands again, and walk in the park. He'd even thought maybe she would want to spend time with him.

Maybe.

The way Frederick felt now, looking into the faces of hundreds of strangers, he knew that, despite everything, he loved her. Beyond reason.

He got a call from Samuel, and they met at the end of the bridge.

"No sign of her?" he asked.

Frederick shook his head. "Look at the notes," he said. "Does that mean she's killing herself? Or what? I don't know. I can't process anything right now." He thrust the notes into Samuel's hand.

Samuel scanned them quickly. "I don't know. It could just be that she's leaving. It could be... the other thing. Freddie, we should call the cops to see if they know anything. Maybe she's..." He trailed off.

They both knew what image they had in their heads – that she'd jumped already, and police were on the scene, or she'd been rushed to hospital.

"Yeah," Frederick said hoarsely. "I'll call them."

"No, I'll do it," Samuel said.

Frederick appreciated his brother's offer, and nodded, a lump in his throat. Even as they talked, he was still watching every woman that passed by, hoping and wishing and praying to any god that would listen that it would be Helen.

He'd been seriously considering divorcing her, but now? He wanted to give it another try. He had to, if she was found.

Frederick had no idea she'd been depressed. He knew how depressed he was. He'd been to a doctor for it who'd prescribed antidepressants for him. Helen never let on she was feeling anything other than glee at drinking every night at her job and otherwise being out of the house with her friends whenever she could.

Usually it was just him and the kids for most of the weekend, and he was always beyond grateful any time she deigned to return home before they went to bed. The kids rarely asked where she was, because being with Dad was their normal. It was Frederick they cried for in the middle of the night when they were sick. They hadn't even cried for her that morning. They'd cried because Frederick had been so different from his usual calm, collected self.

"Nothing," Samuel said as he ended the call to the police. It was only then that Frederick realized how zoned out he'd been. He hadn't even heard any of the conversation his brother had with the police.

"Let's check every single bridge, everywhere, just in case," Frederick said. "And we need to go where she works. Maybe she wanted to do it, but then decided not to."

"The bar where she works won't be open right now," Samuel said. "I think it's unlikely she'd be able to do…. It… at this hour, you know, with everyone around. Maybe you're right. Maybe she went out this morning with the intention of doing it, but then thought better of it. We should check your apartment to see if she's gone back there. If she's not there, then we need to think of where else she could be and go to each and every one of those places."

"Yes, I agree." He called her cell again, but there was no answer. "Let's go to the apartment. Now," he said.

CHAPTER FIVE

A couple of days after their talk at Kat's, Kat called Marion and asked if she could come to her home.

"If I'm going to track your husband down," she'd said over the phone, "I need to learn everything I can about him."

"Yes," Marion had said quietly. "Although…"

"Although?"

"Although I can't help wondering if he really is dead, and the note was just malicious."

"It could have been," Kat had agreed.

"It's just impossible to tell," Marion said. "Come over, anyway, so I can show you everything I have about Richard."

Kat headed over to her home early the next morning. She and Lacie were taking Florence to the petting zoo that afternoon, so she wanted to be back at her house in plenty of time.

She had a quick omelette breakfast that Blaine cooked. His bacon and cheese omelette was one of Kat's favorite breakfasts. Then they both headed out the door, kissed on the driveway, and left in their separate cars, Blaine to work, and Kat to Marion's.

Marion's home was on the outskirts of Lindsay, a twenty-minute drive from where Kat lived. It was on an idyllic street lined with trees. Since so many of the homes had brick facings, it reminded Kat a little of England. Marion lived in a large symmetrical home with a wraparound porch and a red brick façade.

The yard was charming. A climbing plant sprawled over the front of the house, draping a little where it shouldn't over the windows, and creeping out at odd angles, but in its slightly untamed state it looked beautiful. Flowers bloomed everywhere, but weeds crept alongside them, too. The lawn was slightly overgrown, but still showed evidence of having been mowed not too long ago.

From its appearance, Kat guessed it had once been immaculate, but since Richard had been gone, it was probably harder to maintain things. As she pulled into the driveway, Kat thought that was probably the case with Marion. She'd once been immaculately groomed and full of smiles. Now it was a strain for her to maintain that appearance.

The front door opened before Kat got to it, as if Marion had been waiting at the window, watching for her.

"Good morning, Kat," Marion said. She smiled, but it was small and sad and didn't light up her eyes.

"Morning, Marion." Kat surprised herself by walking over to her and hugging her. She hadn't planned on doing that, but Marion looked like she needed one.

Marion hugged her tightly for a moment, then stepped away from the embrace, dabbing at her eyes. "Come in, come in. Would you like a cup of coffee? Tea?"

"Coffee would be wonderful, thank you. Cream and sugar if you have it."

"I always have coffee. In fact I find myself drinking way too much these days. Why don't you come back to the kitchen with me?"

As they walked along a hallway leading to the kitchen, Kat saw a large family photo on the wall. Marion looked gorgeous in it, with her hair freshly coiffed and skimming her shoulders. She had a huge smile and the light of a truly satisfied woman was in her eyes. Richard had his arm around her protectively.

Their four children sat in front of them, two girls and two boys, all looking just as happy. Kat's heart sank. What a wonderful family and now it had been torn apart. Whatever had happened was tragic, whether he was missing or dead.

Marion led her into a large room, which had a kitchen on one side and a living room on the other. A young teenaged girl was sprawled out on a couch, asleep.

"Betsy's having a bit of an episode at the moment," Marion said, nodding towards her. "I kept her home from school today. She gets like this so often they send work home for her. She's supposed to be doing it now. The thing is, she doesn't have any energy. She's able to concentrate for about fifteen minutes at a time, then... well, you can see what happens."

"Poor girl," Kat said. "Are her medications helping?"

"Not so far," Marion said as she headed over to the coffee maker and switched it on. "The doctors are pretty much guessing right now. At first they thought it might be multiple sclerosis, and so did we. But that doesn't seem to be what's wrong with her. We're just not sure right now, so it's test after test after test."

"That sounds like it would be very stressful on all of you."

"It is, but I can take that. I just worry about her so much. How is she going to hold down a job? Have an independent life? Have children? And if she can't, how frustrating will that be for her? She has all her mental faculties. She's just a normal girl in that way, so she'll want to go to the prom, college, and do everything everyone else does. But will she be able to? That's what I keep asking myself."

All Kat could do was nod sympathetically. She didn't have an answer. There were no answers.

Marion busied herself getting the coffee ready. "Kat, I've been meaning to tell you something," she said, not looking her in the eye.

"Hmm?"

"I was wondering, and I know this might sound really silly to you. Maybe it's just something that happens only in the movies. I was wondering, well, could it be possible that Richard hit his head when he was whitewater rafting and that he didn't die, like people thought, but instead he got amnesia? Maybe he doesn't remember who he is or who we are, and he's out there somewhere."

"I don't know much about it, Marion. I'm not a doctor, but I suppose it could be possible. Let me Google it." She did and found that indeed, it would be possible.

The article said, "*Retrograde amnesia is the term for the inability to recall information that was acquired before a particular date, usually the date of an operation or accident,*" she read. "*Most traumatic brain injuries only lead to concussion, a temporary and mild condition. However, a severe injury such as a serious blow to the head, can damage areas in the brain responsible for memory storage, which can lead to retrograde amnesia.*

"Yes, Marion, it looks like that is a possibility."

Marion nodded. "I went down to the place where he did the whitewater rafting. There are so many rocks and boulders there. The place is just covered with them and some of them have pretty sharp edges.

"He could easily have been thrown out of the raft, knocked his head on a boulder, and landed on another rock or on the bank. Then, maybe he woke up a little later, no one realized he was missing, and he could have made his way somewhere. Maybe he's living a totally new life right now, with no memory of us."

"Maybe," Kat said.

Marion gave Kat her coffee and sipped from her own. "Now, let me show you everything I have of him. I've put it all together in our main living room. This way."

Kat followed her into the living room, which was gorgeous, warm and homely. It was decorated in a red-themed wallpaper with red, orange, and purple cushions. Mexican throws were casually tossed over the back of the couches. Books, papers, photo albums and a number of other family memorabilia things had been spread out on the rug.

"Would you like to sit on the couch, and I'll bring them to you?" Marion asked.

"Oh no, no," Kat said. "I'll sit on the floor. It'll be much easier that way."

They spent a long time poring over everything. Kat learned that Richard loved sports, the more extreme the better. Privately, she thought it was a miracle he hadn't died earlier, given all the cliffs he'd jumped off and planes he'd leaped out of. Still, she knew she was a little prejudiced in that area.

She couldn't stand the idea of extreme sports and had absolutely no idea why anyone would be crazy enough to deliberately put themselves in danger. Still, she was mature enough to know that other people loved it, and she'd learned to simply let them be. But even though she tried, she couldn't understand the attraction.

She also learned that Richard loved his work. He was a management and strategy consultant, working independently, who went into various businesses around the state, and basically, in Marion's words, "told them what they were doing wrong and how they could fix it."

Marion explained he was more hands-on than other consultants, and sometimes stayed with a company for three or four years in a consulting capacity, becoming a real part of their team and implementing new ideas. He'd been offered a permanent position with many of these companies over the years, but he'd never accepted one. "He liked his freedom too much," Marion said.

When she put the pieces of information together, Kat got a picture of Richard as a man who loved new ideas, thrills, and challenges. He certainly wasn't the kind of guy to get a job, stick with it for fifty years, and be happy drawing a regular paycheck, and later, a pension.

She voiced these thoughts to Marion, who agreed with a laugh. "No, he'd have said a life like that would kill him inside."

"How did it affect you? Were you comfortable with his risk taking?" Kat knew she was probably projecting a little. In all honesty, she'd have found being married to a man like Richard difficult. She liked her men a little more dependable, steady, and less full of surprises. And that was before even getting to the extreme sports!

"Oh, I loved it!" Marion said, her eyes lighting up. "The kids did, too. He'd do the craziest things for us. Like, this one time, he booked a trip to Disney World at the very last minute. Then he told me to come along while he took the kids to school, so he could show me something in the office. And so I did.

"And, would you believe, he'd packed all our bags during the night and loaded them into his truck. We had an absolute monster of a truck back then, so even on the way there, we still didn't notice anything.

"Then we took a wrong turn, and one of the kids told him that wasn't the way to school. And he said, 'Yes, I know. Because we're not going to school, we're going to the airport. We're going to Disney World!'"

"Wow!" Kat said. "That's quite something."

"It was amazing," Marion said, still breathing with happiness. "He was amazing." Then her eyes clouded over, and her face crumpled.

Kat felt for her. "I'll do the best I can, Marion. Really, I will," she said reassuringly.

"Thanks, Kat. Oh, and one other thing. I wanted to get into his emails to see if there are any clues there, but I don't have his password."

"Yes, that would help," Kat said. "Maybe if you look through his things, he might have written it down somewhere."

"I have," Marion said. "I haven't had any luck so far, but I'll keep searching."

"Please do," Kat agreed. "We need to find something to go on. For right now, I'm going to go home and think about all this."

"Sure."

"One thing I need to ask you. Do you know where he kept his passport?"

Marion nodded. "Yes. It's in the drawer upstairs, where he always kept it."

CHAPTER SIX

"Ahh, here's to Caribbean life!" Michael Tomlinson said, lifting his glass of rum punch.

"Indeed!" his fiancée Rebecca Norman said. "The sun, the sea, the breeze. What could be better?"

They were at a hotel restaurant overlooking the Caribbean Sea, watching the waves that glittered in the tropical light of the early afternoon. It was an exclusive hotel nestled into a steep mountainside, a real feat of architecture. They often came there, enjoying the wonderful Creole food, friendly service, and, of course, the view. They usually went to the spa first for a couples' massage, so by the time they were eating they were thoroughly relaxed.

They were a very sociable couple, and often struck up a conversation with guests who were staying at the hotel and eating in the restaurant. Today was no different, and they had started talking with two men from Canada who had come to the island on business. The two men, Jonas and Trevor, were architects and had been sent down by their firm to design a large office complex in town.

Jonas, a tall, slim African-Canadian with a charming smile and wonderful bone structure, so wonderful he could have been a model, said, "Tell us more about your business idea."

Michael was happy for the invitation to do so. His mind swelled with possibilities and the heady excitement of it all. "This place is such a beautiful island. So romantic. A real getaway for couples."

Rebecca squeezed his hand and gave him a loving, affectionate glance.

"We want other couples to experience the joy and romance we're experiencing," he continued. "We've bought a piece of land not too far from here. It's a little off the beaten track, but it's just exquisite."

"It is," Rebecca said. "The views over the sea are marvelous, and it's so quiet and peaceful. A real slice of paradise."

Trevor, an older man with a large pot belly and a friendly manner, nodded. "It sure is an escape from the bustle of Toronto."

"I'll say," added Jonas. "I know my wife would be all over a romantic vacation here on the island."

"Perhaps you'll be our first customers," Michael said with a laugh. "We're planning on constructing little villas, here and there, dotted throughout the property, each with its own veranda. Just small villas, with a large living and sleeping space."

"And beautiful outdoor showers," Rebecca added.

"We'll have a communal infinity pool and a little restaurant," Michael said. "We're not into cooking ourselves, so we'll employ a local to cook wonderful Caribbean food for our guests."

"It sounds like a dream," Jonas said.

"That's our goal," Michael said. "We're just looking into the ins and outs of it now. The costs, logistics, all of that. I was a hotelier back in Oklahoma, but this is a totally different landscape, as I'm sure you can imagine."

"Well, you'd better take our phone numbers," Trevor said. "The next time we come we'll stay there and bring our spouses along. What do you say, Jonas?"

"I say cheers to that," Jonas clinked his glass with the others.

They finished their desserts, talking about where the best beaches were, and the best things to do on the island. Then they exchanged numbers, paid their respective bills, and headed their separate ways.

Michael and Rebecca walked hand in hand up the walkway to the parking lot. Bougainvilleas bloomed all around them in bright fuchsia, soft pink, and dazzling white.

"Those men were nice," Rebecca said.

"Yes, they were," Michael said. His smile stretched into a cheeky grin. "Though I do love it when it's just you and me."

She gave him a quick hug as they walked. "Oh you, you're so romantic."

"Not at all," he said. "Just telling the truth. And nothing but the truth. I can't wait until we're married."

"Nor can I," Rebecca said. "I just hope…" She made wide eyes and they both knew what she was talking about.

"Don't worry," Michael said soothingly. "It will all be absolutely fine."

She looked at him with wide and innocent big brown adoring eyes. "Promise?"

"I promise," he said, though he really couldn't do any such thing.

"Let's think about happy things," she said. "Like on the beach in the evening, barefoot. With a steel pan band."

"Are you sure about the steel pan band, honey? It's a little déclassé.”

“It’s a little what?” she said, sounding annoyed.

“Nothing, nothing,” he said quickly. “What would you like them to play?”

“Romantic songs,” she said. “Maybe…” She burst into song. “*Said I loved you but I lied! This is more than love I feel inside.*”

Privately, Michael didn’t like that song. He’d thought it cheesy when it had come out in the early 90s, and it had only gotten worse with the passing of time. But he’d never tell Rebecca that. He wanted her to be happy, no matter what. He fixed a smile on his face. “That would be wonderful, honey.”

“It would, wouldn’t it?” They reached the parking lot and she wrapped her arms around his neck. “Oh, Michael! I’m so, so glad I met you.”

Michael smiled back at her pretty face. “I’m happy, too.”

“Happy? Only happy?” Rebecca asked, looking put out.

“Overjoyed!” he said, laughing. “I never expected you to come along out of the blue. But you did. And now I can say I’m the happiest man alive.”

“Me too,” Rebecca said. “Well, the happiest woman alive. We know how to love, how to care for each other, and…” She grinned saucily. “There’s certainly nothing lacking in the bedroom department.”

“Oh, really?” he said. “Care to test that statement out when we get home?”

“I’d love to.” She winked at him, then got into the passenger side of their white Honda sedan. “Step on the gas, honey.”

Michael got in the car and they drove out of the hotel grounds. It was a winding road, up hills, down valleys, left to right, right to left, all the way home. Michael swung round corners with ease, his sunglasses on, his left arm leaning against the door, where the window was open. He felt like a million bucks.

Soon they arrived in their hometown, which was called Martine, after the Martine Estate which had once been situated on the very spot where the town was now located. It was a rural area, which was just transitioning from an agricultural hub into a high-end residential area with lots of newly built expensive homes. The land values were skyrocketing.

Michael, having been quite shrewd, had managed to buy a large piece of land on the outskirts of town at a low price, which had a small house on it. The lot stretched back for eight acres from the street, slightly undulating for the first seven acres, then down a modest sized hill all the way to a ravine at the bottom, which made up the last acre. The ravine was the property boundary.

He planned to sell off two lots next to the frontage road at prices so high they'd cover the initial purchase price he'd paid and more, then use the proceeds to pump into their romantic development. He already had some money stashed away, but any extra funds were always welcome.

They were also planning to renovate the house. It was perfectly fine the way it was, but Rebecca wanted the best, and Michael wanted to give her nothing but the best. So that was another expensive project in the works.

Michael's heart filled with joy and excitement every time they made the last turn on the road to Martine and then entered the outskirts of the town. This time was no exception, as he could feel the excitement building as he drove towards their home.

They had the car windows down, and birds chirped in the trees as they drove along the road. The sky was a perfect blue, and the breeze was blowing gently, a welcome relief from the heat. Their house was picturesque, painted in light powder blue and light turquoise. There were palm trees swaying gently next to the house and vivid flowers flourished in the beds in front of the porch.

"Ahh," Rebecca sighed, satisfied. "Home, sweet home."

Michael smiled at her as he pulled the Honda to a stop. "I don't think we're ever going to get tired of saying that, are we?"

Rebecca smiled back, but as her eyes tracked over to the house, her smile immediately dropped from her face. Her brow furrowed. She looked disturbed. "Michael, what's…" Suddenly her voice shook with urgency. "Michael!"

Michael turned to look at the house. His heart dropped into his feet. He quickly got out of the car. "Stay here," he said.

There, on the steps leading to the house, was the most horrific sight.

A huge dead pig was lying on their porch steps. And it was no accident. Blood streamed from the pig, onto the walkway. Written in blood on the concrete, was one single word *LEAVE*.

Michael looked at it, turned around, and threw up in the flowers.

CHAPTER SEVEN

"Does Richard come from around here?" Lacie asked. "Well, I mean, Lindsay."

They were at the petting zoo, which was forty-five minutes outside Lindsay, hence Lacie's self-correction.

"No," Kat said. "He's from Morrisey."

"Not that far from here."

They were sitting on a picnic bench, while Florence was petting some goats under the supervision of a zoo staffer. She'd been doing it for a long time and really seemed to love the little goats. Lacie and Kat had done all the usual photo-taking and laughing and saying how cute she was, but they couldn't get her to leave the goats.

She wasn't even tempted by the ice cream Lacie bought for her, which was absolutely shocking, since Florence adored ice cream, particularly strawberry ice cream.

She'd latched on to one particular little goat, who had a black coat and white spots on his forehead and nose. Jeremiah was his name which Kat and Lacie found inordinately funny for some reason. They were in quite a giggly mood anyway, and Florence had taken to chasing him around, squealing with delight.

"Morrisey is about an hour's drive from Lindsay," Kat said. "His mother is still alive. His father passed away a long time ago."

Lacie shook her head in mock-disdain. "Uh, Mom? Hello? That should be your first port of call. His mom."

"What makes you say that?"

"Mother's instinct," Lacie said. "She'll know if her son is alive or not. Right now, she'll think he's dead, of course, because she doesn't know about the note. But I'll bet if you tell her about the note, she'll get a hunch either way."

"Hm..." Kat said. "I don't know, Lace. That's pretty dicey. I know people put a lot of stock in hunches, and I do think there's probably something to be said for intuition. For example, if you see a person and you instantly have a bad feeling, that may have some merit. But our judgments can be skewed by so many other things."

Lacie didn't look convinced. "One sec." Florence's ice cream had dripped down onto Lacie's hand. "Florence, ice cream!" Lacie called over cheerily to Florence, but obviously Jeremiah was much more interesting than Mommy, and Florence ignored her. Lacie shrugged and smiled. "All the more for me then." She took a lick of Florence's ice cream cone, then another, and another.

"Think about people with anxiety for example," Kat continued. "Or people who've been through some kind of trauma. They might be on a high-alert more than other people, which would skew their judgment. They'd see danger, when no real danger was there."

"That's an extreme example, Mom," Lacie said.

"Is it? For one, many people do suffer from anxiety. So maybe it came from that. We can't always be right about things all the time."

Lacie grinned. "I can, and I am," she said decisively. Then she laughed. "No, I get what you mean, Mom. I just think you're wrong. I think you're talking about the exceptions to the rule."

"Maybe," Kat said. "Anyway, I guess it's worth a try. She might have some information Marion doesn't have. Marion told me she lives in a tiny little community right outside Morrisey. I think I'll just show up and find out where her house is."

"Good plan," Lacie said.

Kat, feeling relaxed now that she'd decided on her next move for the investigation, went back to watching Florence. "She's really fascinated with Jeremiah, huh?"

"Yep," Lacie said. "Maybe she'll be a goat farmer when she gets older." She took the last bite of the ice cream and laughed. "Oh, well. Snooze you lose, Florrie. Just kidding. I'll buy her another one, of course. I just think it's better that we let her enjoy herself."

"With all that running after Jeremiah, she's going to have a great nap in the car on the way home," Kat said.

Lacie laughed. "Yep. Though I really don't want her to nap at the moment, since I'm going back to work so soon. I want to spend every waking moment with her." The light in Lacie's eyes dulled a little.

"Don't feel guilty," Kat said. "You're doing what you know is right."

Lacie held her head high. "Yes. I am. You're right. Argh. Mom-guilt. Does it ever go away?"

"Nope," Kat said. "Sorry, kiddo. I always worry about you, even though you're absolutely fine. In fact, your life is turning out absolutely wonderful. Still, I fret a little from time to time. I think I hide it pretty well, though, don't I?"

"You do, to be fair," Lacie said. "I don't get it, though. I'm not in any trouble or anything. Why worry?"

Kat sighed. "If I knew, I'd tell you, honey."

"Can I tell you a secret?" Lacie asked. "Tyler jokes that I'm ridiculous. I still check Florence's breathing sometimes when she's sleeping. I know she's way past the SIDS age now. Just, sometimes the urge overtakes me. I've got it down to only once a week or so."

"Perfectly normal," Kat said with a smile, "but you know you don't have to."

"I know," Lacie said. "Ugh. I just didn't know I'd love her this much. Since I've had her, I'm starting to realize how much you love me, and how much you did for me when I was a kid. I mean, I always knew you loved me, but now I know you love me, love me."

Kat laughed. "Very eloquent, Lace, and I mean that sarcastically."

"You knew what I meant," Lacie said, rolling her eyes.

"I did," Kat said. "And I'm glad you know." She took Lacie's hand, but then pulled her own hand back. "Yuck, it's all sticky!"

"Ice cream does drip, you know?" Lacie said with a snicker. "The paper napkin wasn't much help. I'll just have to wash my hands."

They rounded up Florence, who whined a little when separated from Jeremiah, but was soon placated with her own strawberry cone. Then they went over to where some little lambs were, and when Florence was finished petting them, it was time to go home.

Kat headed out to Morrisey that afternoon, going to the little community just outside the town where Marion had told her Mrs. Molesey lived. She asked a man who was standing on a corner if he knew where she might be able to find the house.

A few minutes later she was parking on the street in front of the house. There was a driveway, but she thought it might be considered aggressive of her to park there, since the woman didn't even know she was coming.

The house where Richard's mother lived was an old-style white single-story home with a wraparound porch, complete with the obligatory rocking chair on it. There was no front yard to speak of, simply a driveway and a tiny patch of grass. There were no plants out front, and the only decoration was a wind chime hanging from the porch ceiling.

Kat took a deep breath, steeling herself. She had to be quite careful, she realized. This woman believed her son had died in a tragic accident, and for all Kat knew, maybe he had died in a tragic accident. She didn't want to get the woman's hopes up in case her son really was dead.

As it turned out, Mrs. Molesey didn't seem to be the worrying mother type.

She opened the door after Kat knocked, and looked her up and down. "Are you a Jehovah's Witness? Because if you are…"

"I'm not," Kat said with a smile.

"Good for you, because I was going to slam the door on you. In fact, I'm still going to slam the door on you unless you've got a very good story. I'm counting down. Three…"

"My name's Kat Denham."

"Two…"

"I know your daughter-in-law, Marion, from my tennis club."

"She hasn't sent you to come begging for money, has she?"

Kat was shocked, but tried not to let it show on her face. Didn't she want to support and help her grandchildren? "No…"

"Good. One…"

"We've had some information about Richard," Kat blurted out. "He may not be dead after all. Well, we don't really know."

Mrs. Molesey paused for a moment. "Who's we?"

"Marion got a note."

"A note?" She made it sound ridiculous. In fact, her whole manner seemed designed to make Kat feel like a schoolgirl being scolded.

But Kat was made of tougher stuff. "Yes, a note. I was wondering if you had any ideas about where he might have gone, if he is alive."

"Don't know," she said. "Wouldn't surprise me, though. He was always a selfish kid. Gosh darned selfish, as soon as he came out of the womb, he was. Cried and cried and cried and wouldn't stop, no matter what you did for him.

"Didn't improve any as he got older, like everyone said he would." She rolled her eyes. "Just got worse and worse. Had to throw him out of the family home when he was fifteen. He started being nasty to my Gregory. And no one's nasty to my Gregory."

"Gregory?"

"My son." Mrs. Molesey laughed at Kat. "You come around here poking your nose in my affairs, and you didn't even know Richard had a brother?"

Marion hadn't told Kat that.

"Anyway, Gregory," Mrs. Molesey said, cheering up, like they'd hit on her favorite subject. "That's a young man worth looking into. You know, he was made partner in a prestigious law firm in New York at the age of thirty-two? Isn't that quite something? And he always sends me the most wonderful Christmas presents, and comes to visit as often as he can. Richard, living just a short drive away, however… Well, the less said about him, the better."

"I hope you don't mind me saying this," Kat said. "But you don't seem to care much that he's died."

"Frankly, my dear," she said in such a patronizing way it made Kat quite annoyed, "it's a blessed relief. He was an embarrassment. Let's say he's dead. Well, he was selfish, wasn't he? Whitewater rafting when he had a family, well, something like a family, back home."

Kat got the impression Mrs. Molesey did not approve of Marion or the kids. Perhaps just by their connection to Richard. "And if he didn't die. What? He faked his own death? Selfish. As usual."

"We were thinking he might have gotten amnesia from a head injury and lost his memory."

"Well, now, wouldn't that be something? Perhaps it would do that hard head of his some good to get knocked. Maybe some sense might get knocked into it."

"Right," Kat said. She was beginning to feel rather sorry for Richard, whether he was alive or dead.

"Gregory, on the other hand… You'd be much better spending your time thinking about him."

"Well, maybe I should go speak to him," Kat said. "About Richard."

"No point," Mrs. Molesey said. "They haven't spoken in twenty years. Got good sense, my Gregory. Stays away from bad company, even if it is his own blood."

Kat was just stunned by her attitude. "Was Richard in contact with you any time before he went missing?"

"Was he in contact?" Mrs. Molesey mocked her. "No. He wasn't. Too selfish to give his own mother a call before he died."

"It was an accident," Kat said. It seemed Richard would get blamed by her for every hurricane, earthquake and tsunami, too.

"You just said maybe it's not."

"Yes, but... Never mind," Kat said. "Anyway, thank you for your time, Mrs. Molesey."

"Yeah," the woman said. As she closed the door, Kat heard her say, "Shoulda' been a Jehovah's Witness, after all. Woulda' been a better use of my time."

Kat went back to her car, still shocked. She'd never heard anyone speak about their own child the way Mrs. Molesey spoke about Richard. It was quite surreal and slightly unnerving.

She drove home and decided to put it all out of her mind for the evening. She walked into the kitchen, thinking about what she'd make for dinner, and found Blaine with his sleeves rolled up, his hands and entire forearms covered in flour and dough. He even had a smudge of flour on his nose. He grinned at her.

"Hello, darling," she said. "Looks like we're in for a treat tonight."

"I sincerely hope so," he said. "I'm trying to replicate that spinach and feta calzone we had when we went to visit Deborah and Luigi in Italy. But I have to warn you, there's a slight chance it might fail miserably."

"That's what I like," Kat said. "A cook who isn't afraid to try something new."

He smiled. "Well, the Chinese takeout is on speed dial number two, so I have a backup plan. There's a glass of wine for you on the table."

"Thank you. I could use one," Kat said. She picked up the glass of white wine and sipped it. "Very nice indeed. What is it?"

"A Sauvignon Blanc I picked up when I was getting the groceries," Blaine said. "I managed to get everything wrapped up early today, so I thought I'd surprise you."

"Thank you, darling," Kat said. She came over and gave him a kiss on the cheek.

"I won't hug you," he said, "or you'll get dough all over your outfit."

"Appreciated," Kat said with a chuckle. "Now, this gives me a perfect opportunity to get some writing done. Is it all right with you if I sit at the kitchen table, and we just work alongside each other companionably? Or would you rather chat?"

"The former," he said. "If we get too deep into conversation, our chances we'll be eating Chinese takeout tonight will increase exponentially. I'm following directions very carefully."

Kat smiled. "All right, District Attorney Evans."

Blaine winked. "Better than all right, Sexy Cissy."

CHAPTER EIGHT

The weekly woman's tennis social rolled around again, and as they had the last time, they met in the clubhouse. Mitzi had an urgent last minute booking for an important client, so she had to skip it, but Lennon was there, looking sunny and happy as usual. "I'm determined to get better," she said, and Kat admired her sportsmanship.

There was one key difference this time, though. There was a man in front of the clubhouse, pruning some flowers. He was about fifty, and in Kat's opinion, quite a silver fox!

He gave Lennon and Kat a friendly smile on their way in, and they returned it. If Mitzi had been there, she and Kat would have shared a look about how good-looking he was, but she knew Lennon didn't go in for that sort of thing.

When it was time to get started, Glenys said, "I see there are no new members today. Well, ladies, we all know each other, and we're becoming quite the little group, aren't we?"

Susie took their lunch orders, then reached into her bag, "Darn it! I left the tennis balls in my car. I'll be back in a minute." She dashed out to the parking lot, while the others wandered onto the courts.

Marion was talking to Glenys, looking more animated than usual, which Kat was glad to see.

Lennon and Kat chatted about this and that while they were doing some gentle stretches at the same time as they waited for Susie to return.

"How is your lovely family?" Lennon asked.

Kat smiled. "Florence is doing just wonderful. We went to the petting zoo yesterday, and she became pretty attached to a little goat called Jeremiah, chasing him around the place for what seemed like ages. It was the first time we'd ever gone there, but we'll definitely have to go again."

"Oh, yes, my little ones love the petting zoo. Perhaps we can all go sometime."

"That would be fantastic," Kat said. "I'll be watching Florence on Mondays and Thursdays while Lacie's at work. She has Friday off, and then Florence is in daycare Tuesdays and Wednesdays."

"That'll be nice," Lennon said. "She'll get a wide range of experiences and settings. And the two of you will be thick as thieves, no doubt."

Kat smiled. "Yes. I'm very much looking forward to it. Lacie's feeling a little guilty that she can't be with Florence full time, but I keep reassuring her everything will be just fine."

"It will," Lennon said decisively.

"How is your family, Lennon?" Lennon had seventeen-year-old twins, Jethro and Candace, fifteen-year-old Susannah, and a ten-year-old boy named Gideon, the one who was amazing at baking. Then there was a large age gap, followed by three-year-old Esther and two-year-old Abigail.

"Just great, thank you," she said. "Abigail's starting to say many more words, although she's been babbling at Esther since she was six months old. Somehow they seem to understand each other."

Kat grinned. "I think it's a secret baby language."

"I agree," Lennon said with a laugh. "Gideon's given up his competitive trampolining, which is a little sad, but he's taken up a pastry baking course instead. Susannah's still training every day for the state trampolining championships next month. Candace is looking at colleges for next year. She wants to study geology.

"Jethro's not sure where he wants to go yet, or what he wants to do. He's still helping with the worship band and thinking about Bible College. We'll have to see. He's also toying with the idea of computer programming of some kind. He's into computer science and all that complex coding stuff, whatever that is."

Kat smiled and shook her head. "Your family is something else, Lennon. Always so busy and fruitful. They must be an inspiration to all their friends."

"I hope so," Lennon said. "The most important thing, of course, is that they're happy. Which they are, thank goodness."

"Yes," Kat said. "That's true."

When Susie came back from her car and handed them their tennis balls, she said, "Kat, you go with Glenys. Marion, you go with Lennon. I'll hang back for this round, then we'll rotate. That way someone will get a welcome rest each time."

They all laughed, but Lennon looked wide-eyed at Kat. She was the worst player, Marion being the best. "I'm going to get thrashed," she whispered in Kat's ear.

Kat couldn't disagree. "Just try your best. I think playing against great players helps you up your game, because they can't help but put pressure on you."

"That's true," Lennon said, then she smiled. "Thanks, Kat, that was a great positive reframe." Lennon was all about putting a positive spin on everything.

"Go get it," Kat said with a laugh.

Their games got underway. Kat was improving, and gave Glenys, a good player, a run for her money. She was on a break next, then played with Lennon, who was still as dreadful as ever, but remained cheerful. She had a lively game against Marion, in which she managed to hold her own, but eventually lost, then had a pretty even match with Susie.

By the time they were finished playing, they were hot and happy as they headed back to the clubhouse for drinks and sandwiches.

As they walked past the gardener, Marion said, "Hello, Graham," to him, so cheerfully and brightly, he looked shocked. Kat guessed it was because the before-tennis-Marion and the after-tennis-Marion were entirely different creatures.

He smiled back, a light in his eyes that let Kat know he was "interested" in Marion and said, "Hi there, Marion. I saw you were stunning as ever on the courts today. Are you ever going to give anyone else a chance to win?" His wide smile and mischievous eyes made him look even more attractive.

Marion blushed. "Well, everyone's got to be good at something."

When they went inside, Kat grinned at Marion. "Do I detect a little romance?"

"Oh no, nothing of the sort," Marion said, not meeting Kat's eyes. "It's far too soon for me to move on, and I've got a family to think of. Speaking of which, how are things going?"

Kat told her all about her meeting with the elder Mrs. Molesey.

Marion's eyes widened. "I'm so sorry," she said. "I haven't spoken to her in some time. But I am surprised, because I didn't know she felt that badly about us."

"She's the one missing out," Kat comforted her. "I don't know about Richard, since I never met him, but you're a lovely, kind woman. A good person."

"Thank you, Kat," she said.

"Oh," Kat said, as an idea suddenly popped into her head. "You said you wanted to get into Richard's email."

"Yes, I want to see if there are any clues as to what's going on."

"What about Lennon's son, Jethro?" Kat mused. "Lennon says he's really into computers and programming and all of that. Maybe he can find a way to get in."

"I don't know if that's a good idea," Marion said, "I don't want to trouble them."

"I don't think they'd feel that way at all," Kat said. "I'm sure they'd be glad to help. Maybe we can float the idea with Lennon now."

Marion looked at Glenys and Susie. "Not here. Perhaps we can meet privately? Do you think Lennon would come over to my house?"

"I'm not sure," Kat said. "She's very busy. It might be a better idea for us to go over to her house instead."

"If it's not too much of an imposition, that would be fine."

On the contrary, Lennon was delighted at the idea of them coming over. "I'll make sure to get Gideon to whip us up something special."

Later that evening, they were in Lennon's gorgeous and immaculately clean home. The younger kids were in bed, and the older kids milled about, doing their own thing.

Kat, Lennon and Marion sat at the kitchen table. Gideon had baked what he called "gourmet chocolate chip oatmeal cookies" before they'd arrived. They were resting on a cooling rack when they came in, but in a few minutes, he plated them.

"Enjoy!" he said, placing the platter with the cookies on it on the kitchen table, then he brought over small plates for them.

"Thank you very much," Kat said.

"I'd love it if you would try one," Gideon said. "I want to see if you like them."

Lennon laughed and pulled her son into a side-hug. "He says there's nothing better than the joy on people's faces when they taste his work."

"I love to cook, Gideon," Kat said, "so I know what you mean." She took a bite, as did Marion and Lennon. "This tastes heavenly," Kat said. The cookie was warm with the chocolate chips wonderfully melted and perfectly crumbly. "My compliments, Gideon."

"Absolutely lovely," Marion said.

"Thank you," Gideon said. "If you don't mind..." He grinned, then swiped one of the cookies for himself.

Lennon laughed at his departing back. "Use a plate."

He dashed back in the kitchen to get one, then scurried away again, giggling.

They all laughed. They spoke for a while about baking and cooking, and then got down to business.

Marion let Lennon know about the email they wanted to get into, and Kat mentioned Jethro.

"Let me see," Lennon said. "Give me a moment." She went upstairs, and came back a few minutes later with her oldest son, Jethro. He was very tall, well over six feet, and looked like a gentle giant.

"Hello, Ms. Denham," he said. "And pleased to meet you, ma'am. I don't believe we've met."

"No, we haven't," Marion said. "I'm Marion Molesey."

"Good evening, Ms. Molesey."

"Good evening," she said back. "You certainly raise charming children, Lennon."

"She's the best mother anyone could ask for," Jethro said.

Even Kat was impressed by that. From the stories she'd read, it was hard to imagine a seventeen-year-old boy saying something like that.

Jethro sat down and took a cookie. "My mother says you need some help with getting into an email account?"

"Yes," Marion said. "My late husband's."

"I can try," he said. "I'll need access to the computer he usually used to see if I can access any saved passwords, or go back in the cache and see what I can work out. Do you still have it?"

"I do," Marion said. "He used both a laptop and the household computer we all shared."

"Sounds great," Jethro said. "School's over for the year, so whenever you need me, just call. I can come tomorrow, if you'd like?"

Marion smiled. "That would be wonderful."

CHAPTER NINE

Kat had given Marion a ride to Lennon's, since Marion's eldest, Liam, who still lived at home, was having car trouble and needed to borrow her car so he could get to his job as the assistant manager at a bowling alley.

After they'd said their goodbyes to Lennon and the family (and they'd each been persuaded to take along a Tupperware of Gideon's cookies), Kat drove Marion home.

"Thanks for the ride, Kat," Marion said when Kat pulled up in front of Marion's home. "I want you to know how much I appreciate everything you're doing for me. I know you don't have to do any of this, but it means a lot to me."

Kat smiled. "You're welcome, Marion. What would life be like if we didn't help each other when we needed it?"

Marion gave her a small smile and got out of Kat's car.

Kat stayed in the driver's seat, watching until Marion got inside. She opened the front door, stepped inside, and then turned and waved. Kat was about ready to leave when she noticed Marion had left her Tupperware box of cookies on the front seat next to Kat.

She picked up the box of cookies and walked up to the front door to return them to Marion. When she got to the front door, she noticed it was partially open. She decided she'd just push the door open and holler out to Marion that she'd forgotten her cookies, and Kat was bringing them to her.

As she stepped inside the house, she heard angry threatening male voices coming from inside the house. She wondered who it could possibly be since Marion lived alone with her four children. Curious, and concerned for Marion's safety, Kat edged down the front hallway towards where the voices were coming from. She peeked around a corner of the living room only to be greeted by a horrific sight.

There were two gunmen, dressed head to toe in black clothing, their faces covered, guns in hand pointed at Marion's children, who were tied up on the floor. Marion hovered in front of her children, her arms outstretched, trying desperately to shield them from harm.

Liam, the oldest, was still at work, but there was Natasha, eighteen, but looking much younger, with silent tears rolling down her cheeks. Logan, Marion's son who was a little younger than Natasha, was white as a sheet and just staring off into space as if he could somehow make this whole thing go away.

Betsy, the youngest of Marion's children, was holding her chin up defiantly, trying to stare down the attackers, but her shaking hands gave her away.

Kat quickly ducked back into the hallway, made her way outside the house, and then called 9-1-1. When the police dispatcher answered, Kat breathlessly said, "I want to report an armed home invasion that is currently taking place at my friend's home."

She gave the dispatcher the address and was assured by the dispatcher that the police would be arriving at the scene within three or four minutes.

After she ended the call to the police, and hoping that she could in some way help Marion and her children, although she wasn't sure how, Kat snuck back into the house and hid in the hall closet just around the corner from the living room. She could easily hear what was being said in the adjacent room.

"WHERE IS RICHARD?" one of the men bellowed. "I WON'T ASK AGAIN!"

"He's dead," Marion said pleadingly. "I told you that, and the kids have told you that too."

Marion looked around the room desperately, and her gaze finally settled above the mantelpiece. "Look! That's the program from his funeral."

Kat remained in her hiding place in the closet, willing the police to hurry up, as she continued to listen to what was happening in the living room.

There was a long pause and everything was quiet. She assumed one of the gunmen was looking at the funeral program. "A whitewater rafting accident," she heard him say. Kat tried to place his accent. *From a southern state, Texas, perhaps?* She thought. She wasn't quite sure.

Next she heard some mumbling, which sounded like the gunmen talking to each other. Then, without another word they quietly walked out of the living room and calmly left the house through the front door. They walked within inches of Kat's hiding place in the closet and never saw her.

Kat had really wanted the police to arrive and apprehend them, but she wasn't foolish enough to try and stop them from escaping, since they were armed and obviously quite dangerous.

She watched them as they made their way around the nearby street corner. Just a moment or two later, she heard a motorcycle engine firing up, then saw them drive off. With their helmets on, they didn't look like armed robbers. They looked like bikers.

Kat went into the living room, where all the kids were crying.

Marion was untying them. And, just like on the tennis court, this was another place where Marion looked unbelievably strong and unwavering. No tears fell from her eyes as she held her children.

Her entire focus was on comforting them. Even her big sixteen-year-old son climbed into her lap on the floor. They ended up in a big heap, Marion trying to get her arms around the three of them.

Kat went back into the hallway again, not wanting to intrude on their private moment. It was so private and raw, and she knew they needed to be alone. She decided she'd stay as calm and collected as possible, in order to talk to the police, and make some sweet tea for everyone, hoping it would help to calm their nerves.

She went into Marion's kitchen and even though she felt a little like she was an intruder, she decided that was better than interrupting the family to ask if she could use the kitchen. She made five cups of sweet tea, and as she did so, she began to wonder who those men were.

And what did they want with Richard?

Were they linked to his disappearance? Obviously, they hadn't killed or kidnapped him, but they certainly had ill-intent toward him. Maybe he'd faked his own death to get away from them. Or, maybe Richard was involved in something shady. Masked gunmen didn't generally come to the homes of innocent people, asking for them by name. It wasn't a robbery. They hadn't taken anything. If anything, it looked like a hit gone wrong.

So if Richard was involved in shady dealings Marion didn't know about, maybe he'd been killed by another shady party.

Once the cups of tea were ready, she took them into the hallway on a tray, and set them on a side table. She didn't want to disturb Marion and the children yet, and besides, she still wanted time to think, to wonder… who on earth were those men?

But there was no time to think about it, for just then the police arrived with flashing lights and blaring sirens. Kat had been so far away in her thoughts she hadn't even noticed the increasing sound of the approaching sirens.

It turned out to be a couple of officers Kat didn't know. They raced in the house, guns drawn. "Hands in the air!" they yelled at Kat.

Kat did as they asked. "You're too late," she said. "The intruders are gone."

The officers eyed one another.

"You could be an intruder, ma'am," he said. "Don't move and keep your hands in the air. I'll shoot you if I have to!"

"Hey, hey," the other officer said. "Cool down, man. Don't get trigger happy on me, buddy. I don't want to get hauled into court."

"I'm the one who called 9-1-1," Kat said.

Just then Marion and her kids came out of the living room.

"Arms up!" the aggressive cop yelled. "Now!"

The calmer cop said, "Have the intruders left?"

"Yes," Marion said.

"Are you the owner of this house?"

"Yes, sir, and these are my children. This is Kat Denham, my friend. Her husband is District Attorney Evans."

The calm cop looked at the aggressive one meaningfully, as if to say, "See? You almost got us in trouble with important people."

The aggressive cop reluctantly lowered his gun. Kat thought she wouldn't be surprised if down the road she'd hear that he'd gotten involved in a police shooting of some kind. He seemed far too eager to pull the trigger.

"Can you describe the intruders?" the calm one asked. "We can radio in to headquarters and let them know what we're looking for. They'll sound out an alarm for everyone to keep an eye out for them."

"They left on a red motorcycle," Kat said. "A large one, though I'm not very good with the different makes. I know nothing about motorcycles. They were dressed all in black and were wearing bike helmets when they left."

"Do you remember what color the helmets were?" the gentler cop asked.

Kat thought. "Blue and white... or black and red? Honestly, my brain seems like mush right now. I'm really sorry. I want to say one had a blue helmet and one had a white one, but that's really a guess. I couldn't swear to it."

The officers said they'd have to take statements from all of them. Kat offered to make sweet tea for the officers, too, but they declined. They went back into the living room to show the officers what had happened.

When they were finished, Marion said, "Is there any possibility that we could get some police protection? I don't know how my kids are going to sleep tonight."

"We can ask," the gentler cop said, looking doubtful. "But budgets are really tight at the department right now. I'm not sure it'll be approved. Can you go to a hotel?"

Marion was on the brink of tears. "The only hotels in town are very expensive. I'm not sure how I can afford to pay for me and four teenaged children. That would be three rooms. And who knows how long we'd have to stay?"

"I'm a personal friend of Chief Moore," Kat said, "through my husband. I'll put a call into him to see what he can do, Marion. Hopefully he can swing it for you."

"Thank you," Marion said gratefully.

Kat called Chief Moore and he told her he'd be happy to provide police protection for a few days. Marion hugged Kat tightly. "Thank you so much."

"You're welcome," Kat said. "More than welcome. I'm just so sorry about what's happened."

The cops announced that they'd finished their work and were about to leave, when Marion said, "Wait. Can I ask you a question?"

The aggressive cop rolled his eyes, but the kinder cop said, "Sure. What is it?"

"Let's go out in the hallway," Marion said. "Kids, stay here, please."

Kat went along and closed the door to the living room behind them.

The gentler cop smiled, putting his hands in his pockets. "Shoot."

"If someone, say... faked their own death," Marion began. "Would police pursue that? Do police look into that type of a case?"

"Occasionally," the gentler cop said. "But that's usually only when it involves charges of fraud. Most of the time when people fake their own deaths, they change their names, maybe get fake passports, so they can start new lives in another part of the country. They don't want to be traced. So, if they use that new identity for certain things, they can indeed by charged with fraud.

"In reality, these cases are rarely pursued, unless they're a person of interest for another crime. It's expensive to pursue and involves collaboration between different departments across different states, and sometimes even different countries."

"Basically, that's a long-winded way of saying we have more important things to do," the aggressive cop said. "Like catching murderers and robbers."

"I see," Marion said graciously. "Well, thank you."

"Why do you ask?" the gentler cop inquired. "Do you have suspicions about your husband?"

"Not really," she said. "It was just something some friends and I were discussing."

"A complete waste of police time," the aggressive cop said.

"Randy," the gentler cop said in a warning tone. "Well, thank you for your time. Real sorry this had to happen to you. And I'm sure if Chief Moore gave the okay for protection, someone will be over here shortly to park outside the house and keep watch."

"Thank you," Marion said.

When the door was closed, Kat said, "Why didn't you tell them about Richard?"

Marion shook her head. "If he has faked his own death, I don't want him charged with fraud. I know if he has done that, telling them would be a huge betrayal on my part, and at the end of the day, he's still the children's father. I couldn't see him getting fined or going to jail. It would kill them.

"Besides, I don't want the kids to know anything is going on. As far as they know, their father is dead. I don't want them to have any false hopes, especially if it turns out Richard really did pass away in the accident."

"Yes, I agree," Kat said. "It's probably better they don't worry about it, or have false hope, as you say. Would you like me to wait here until the police protection arrives?"

"You don't have to," Marion said. "I'm sure you've got a lot of things to do."

"I'm having dinner with Blaine and Lacie and Tyler," Kat said. "But they'll wait for me."

"Nonsense," Marion said. "Go home. We'll be absolutely fine. Honest."

"Well, if you insist," Kat said. "Send me a message when the police protection arrives. Okay?"

"I will."

CHAPTER TEN

Kat spent the following morning catching up on her writing work. What with she and Lacie making the most of her last week of maternity leave, and working on the investigation, she'd gotten a little behind on her projected word count. She liked to plan how many words she'd write a day, based on her book release schedules.

At the moment, she was writing two books.

Under the name Kat Denham, she was writing a new book in a series that was about an interior designer who traveled around the world on design projects and always seemed to stumble into a murder mystery. This time, the heroine was in an upscale English country house that was being converted into a grand hotel, where she'd been contracted to design each and every room.

But then, the young and ambitious hotel developer was murdered, and there were plenty of suspects. The local townspeople were not enamored with the new project that would no doubt see their village flooded with tourists.

The developer wasn't popular with others in the industry, because of his shady business practices and then there was the problem with his previous lovers, all of whom wanted to see him dead. He was a universally hated figure, which made the murder that much harder to solve. It was extremely fun to write.

The other book was under Kat's romance-erotica pen name, Sexy Cissy. It was to be the first in a new series about five eligible brothers from a very wealthy part of Maine. Their father had gifted each of them shares in his fledgling shipping business when they were babies. The gift turned out to be enormously valuable with the youngest son becoming a millionaire in his own right by the age of six, while the oldest had to wait until he attained the grand old age of ten to see his bank account hit seven figures.

Now, as adults, they'd each gone down different paths. One, Lysander, was an irresponsible playboy, and he was to be her first hero in the book. A sharp-as-nails and impossibly beautiful woman would come to tame him, and her own heart would soften in the process.

She had great fun coming up with romantic names for the brothers. Lysander, Sylvian, Laurence, Ambrose, and Isidore were her final choices. Kat made their mother an artist to account for the flamboyant name selections, although Raphael, Valentine, Cyprian, Florian, and Orlando had almost made the cut, too.

She'd set herself a goal of pumping out four thousand words that morning. She was armed and ready to go with a cappuccino from their coffee maker, a Greek yogurt with berries, and some jazz music playing softly in the background.

When she was about fifteen hundred words into the morning's project, her cell phone buzzed. She cursed herself for not turning it off, wishing she'd avoided the distraction. She picked it up with the intention of calling the person back later, and then powering it down. But when she saw Lennon's name flash on the screen, she was too curious not to answer.

"Hi, Kat," Lennon said, cheery as ever. "I have good news. We're at Marion's, and Jethro has cracked the password on Richard's computer."

"Fantastic! Find any clues?"

"I'm not sure," Lennon said. "We're waiting while Marion goes through it all. She insisted we stay for brunch. Her teens are enjoying playing with Esther and Abigail in the back yard, so we thought why not stay? Plus, I want to keep her company. You didn't tell me what happened yesterday, Kat. It sounds like it was awful."

"I know," Kat said. "I rushed back to have dinner with Blaine, Lacie, and Tyler, and tried to put it out of my mind as much as I possibly could. I didn't tell Lacie or Tyler, either, and only let Blaine know when we went to bed."

"It's just terrible," Lennon said. "I'm so sorry it happened."

"I'm sorry, too," Kat said. "That family has been through enough already, and they sure didn't need something like that to happen. I'm hoping the emails will have a clue in them that can give her closure either way. Marion really deserves that."

"She sure does," Lennon said. "I can't even begin to imagine what she's going through. I'm sure it's tearing her up inside. I'm praying for her, but I'd like to do some more practical things, too."

"You're doing a lot already," Kat said. "Jethro helping on the email is just the thing we needed."

"Hmm, yes," Lennon said. "And are you holding up okay? The events of yesterday must have been pretty traumatizing."

"Me?" Kat said. "I'm fine, I'm fine."

"Are you sure?" Lennon asked. "You seem to have had more than your fair share of dangerous situations."

Kat laughed. "That's what Blaine says, too."

"He must be worried sick."

"Yes, he certainly has his moments of concern." Hearing it from someone else other than Blaine made Kat pause. "However, it's not like I go looking for these situations. They just tend to… well, arise."

"I know what you mean," Lennon said. "However, you do tend *to* get yourself more deeply involved than other people would."

"I…"

"It's your good heart," Lennon interrupted. "You can't stand to see people being falsely accused, or in Marion's case, suffering with not knowing the truth, so you help out. And that's certainly an honorable thing to do, but what if something were to happen to you, Kat? If you were with the police department as a detective, you'd have plenty of protection, a firearm, and all the resources on your side. But you're not. You're acting alone very underprotected."

Kat was about to say she had Jazz and Rudy to protect her, but it sounded rather lame, so she closed her mouth. "I guess I see your point."

"Yes," Lennon said quietly. "Think about it. Maybe you should even think about going professional with it."

Kat laughed. "Be a detective? Oh no, I couldn't possibly. I'm afraid I've been rather spoiled by my self-employed non-routine. Plus, I'm starting to look after Florence a couple of days a week starting next week. I wouldn't have the time for that sort of thing at the moment."

"Perhaps in the future," Lennon said.

"Then I'd be an old lady detective," Kat said with a laugh. "No, Lennon, in all honesty, I don't think I'll be going down that path. But I definitely see your point about the danger and not having the resources and all of that. I have to admit I find it hard to say no when people need help."

"Me, too," Lennon said. "Especially being a Christian and wanting to be of service. Let me tell you a little story that may help. When Jethro and Candace were little, before I had Susannah, I belonged to a women's Bible group.

"It was all quite elaborate, with buffet lunches every month and outreach programs and charity fundraisers. It was really quite something. The woman who ran it, who I shall not name, had created something of a monster for herself. She'd enjoyed it initially, but she soon learned it took a great deal of time to manage and organize."

"I can imagine," Kat said.

"It was all so wonderful and everyone enjoyed it so much that she felt guilty to pack it all in, but nobody else wanted to take over. The woman noticed my organizing skills and began delegating work to me. I saw how much good it was doing for the community, and how burdened she was, so I thought the right thing to do would be to help as much as I could. It was only for a few hours a week, so I thought why not."

"Uh-oh, I think I know what's coming."

Lennon laughed. "Yes. Soon she began sending more and more work my way, until I was totally and utterly swamped. But still I kept going. I thought it was very important work, but pretty soon I had no time for anything else. It was like a full-time job. The twins were suffering. My husband was suffering. The house was suffering, and I was suffering, spinning around like a tornado, trying to get everything done."

"Stressful."

"Intensely. Greg sat me down one night and told me, 'Lennon, this has to stop. You're running yourself ragged.' And, you know, I still fought it. I thought I had to martyr and sacrifice myself to be a good person. To really be a good Christian woman. But I was becoming short tempered and snappy. My thoughts were becoming a little darker in nature, and I was less generous, because I wasn't meeting my own needs."

"I see what you mean."

"I say all this because... Well, I wonder about it sometimes, Kat. You've been through so much, taking on all this investigating work. You've been in some very dangerous situations. You were even hospitalized when that studio producer tried to kill you with the poisonous flowers. And yet, you just bounce back, ready to start again, like it's having no effect on you at all. Surely it must be?"

Kat thought for a moment. "I'm not really sure, Lennon. It's certainly having an effect on my husband."

"Naturally," Lennon said. "But what about you?"

"Honestly? I haven't stopped to think about it all that much."

"Ah. Well, as women I think we have a tendency to do that. To think of what everyone else wants and needs, without considering what we want and need."

Kat was quiet for a moment. "I think you may be right. The thing is, when this first started, it just kind of happened. But it's snowballed, and I really haven't thought about it. I've just gone through the motions..."

"Because it was the right thing to do, just like me and my Bible study group," Lennon said.

"Perhaps," Kat said. "Also, it was something new and quite exciting at first. And it helped me feel like I was making a worthwhile contribution. I was helping society, and the victims of some terrible people."

"Yes," Lennon said. "Which is wonderful. You really have done so much good. But... think about the investigation you're doing for Marion. Of course, we're more than happy to help. But think about it. Why, when she told you about it, did you not tell her to get a private investigator?"

"I don't know, Lennon," Kat said.

Lennon sighed. "I don't want to sound like I'm lecturing you, but the fact of the matter is I have plenty of experience in this sort of thing. Making other people's problems my problems. I would dearly love to fix all the problems of the world, Kat, as I'm sure you would, too. But we're not God. We're only human. We need to know our limits."

"Yes. You can lecture away, Lennon. I think I need to hear it."

"In my experience, those limits are when your life and the life of your family is being impacted." Lennon paused. "Kat, I didn't want to say this, but I think it needs to be said…"

"Go ahead," Kat said. "It's all right. I'm listening."

"Please don't be offended," Lennon said. "I just want to put a new perspective on something I think you may have overlooked."

"I'll try not to be offended," Kat said. "I don't offend that easily."

"The last case you investigated, the one with Marie Moorhead. Someone sent a threatening letter to your home. Yes, you had police presence at your home, but think about this, your granddaughter was in your home at the time. What if something terrible had happened?"

A horrible feeling sunk down into Kat's stomach. "You're right, Lennon." Suddenly she felt quite tearful and awfully guilty. "You know, at the time, I thought what I was doing was necessary, something I had to see through. But looking back on it, I did make the choice to investigate.

"And by making that choice, I put my whole family in the line of fire of some very dangerous people. I didn't see it that way then." Kat felt so consumed by guilt that she felt like she was going to cry. "I have to go, Lennon," Kat said. "Talk to you later."

Tears flowing from the realization of what could have been, Kat went into the guest room upstairs where Lacie and Tyler and Florence had stayed when Florence was first born. There was a framed family photograph of all of them, Kat, Blaine, Lacie, Tyler, and Florence, hanging on the wall. They'd posed for it when Florence was about six months old.

Kat looked at it and cried all the more, realizing what she'd done. How she'd exposed all of them to danger, without even really thinking about it. She now understood that her good intentions had blinded her from her duty to care first and foremost for her family.

Lennon was right, if being a police detective was Kat's job, she'd have all the protection, training, and resources she needed to keep them safe. As it was, she had none of that. She was playing a dangerous game, and for the first time she realized how dangerous it was.

She sat down on the bed in the guest room and cried for quite some time.

Feeling guilty, she decided to cook all of them a fabulous dinner. And, realizing she'd been neglecting her self-care with all that was going on, she decided to book an appointment to have her hair done and for a massage.

But as it turned out, she never made the appointment.

CHAPTER ELEVEN

"Mom, great news!" Lacie said, coming through the door with flushed cheeks. She'd walked over from her new home, pushing Florence's stroller.

"I've been given an extra week off. My boss has to travel to New York for a week to see a family in crisis who used to live here in Lindsay. The child will only see him, not any other therapist, so he's closing the practice for a week. I get to spend another week with Florence!" She was positively beaming.

Kat smiled, looking at the sleeping baby with her caramel colored curls. "It seems the stars are aligning for us, Lace, because I have somewhere to go, and I won't be able to take care of Florence for the two days that I said I would."

"Where are you going, Mom?" Lacie tipped her head to one side. "Are you okay? You look... different. Like you've been thinking of something... deep."

"You know me too well," Kat said. She looked quickly at her watch. "Blaine will be home momentarily, and I want to speak to both of you about it at the same time."

"You're not sick, are you?" Lacie asked, looking panicked.

"No, no, I'm not," Kat quickly said to reassure her. "I'm totally fine."

"That's a relief," Lacie said. "You were scaring me."

"Honestly, it's nothing to be worried about. Where's Tyler?"

"Unfortunately, he had to work late. What is that delicious smell?"

"It's yams stuffed with black beans and bell peppers, and roasted leg of lamb. It's a twist on a Cuban recipe I found," Kat said. "I'm going to put a black bean sauce on top and serve it with stewed carrots and red cabbage."

"Good grief," Lacie said. "It sounds to die for. I'm sure Florence will enjoy it, too. She likes lamb, and yams, for that matter. I'll take Tyler back a portion in a Tupperware. Lamb and yam. That rhymes."

Kat raised an eyebrow as she stirred the cabbage and carrots. "Yes, it does."

"I hate to sound like a spoiled brat," Lacie said. "But…"

"You have been known to in the past," Kat said with a laugh.

Lacie picked up a tea towel and swiped Kat with it around the shoulders. "Mom! What I was going to say was, I know you must have fixed something for dessert. It's not your style to leave that out."

"You'd be right," Kat said. "I have a chocolate mousse cheesecake in the refrigerator."

"Ooh, yes!"

"And we've got a starter of creamy mushrooms with garlic and bacon.

"Mom, you've really gone to a lot of trouble!" Lacie exclaimed.

"What's this all about?" She peered at her mother suspiciously. "Mom, where are you going? Is this your way of breaking some bad news to us at dinner?"

Kat stepped away from the pans and cupped Lacie's face in her hands. "No, Lace, it's not, honestly." She gave her a kiss on the forehead.

"Love you, Mom," Lacie said.

"I love you, too, honey," Kat replied.

It was a nice moment and continued being nice when Blaine got home with a very good bottle of wine. He gave both Kat and Lacie a kiss on the cheek, then tickled Florence's toes.

"Don't," Lacie said. "You'll wake her up and mess with her nap schedule."

"Sorry, Lacie," Blaine said, as he placed the wine on the counter. "A nice Chianti," he said to Kat, looking for her approval.

Kat picked it up. "A Castello di Monsanto Chianti Classico Riserva from Tuscany, 2014."

"It has excellent reviews online," Blaine said.

Kat smiled. "Thank you, darling."

Blaine's eyes tracked over the numerous pots on the stove, and the illuminated oven. "To what do we owe this largesse?"

"That's exactly what I asked," Lacie said. "Admittedly, in a less sophisticated way. But she won't tell me what it's all about. She says she has somewhere she needs to go."

"Oh?" Blaine said, looking at Kat.

"You'll find out when I serve dinner," Kat said. "Let's enjoy our wine."

Blaine and Lacie looked at each other, both of them quite mystified.

"Fine," Blaine said, going over to the breakfront where the wine glasses were stored. He took three out and poured the wine.

"How did work go today, Blaine?" Kat asked.

"Does this having to go someplace have something to do with the investigation you're doing for Marion?" Blaine asked, clearly unable to think of anything else.

Kat sighed, looking between the two of them. "It's obvious neither one of you will be able to concentrate until I tell you. The food will take another five minutes. Can't you wait?"

"Five minutes!" Lacie said. "That seems like forever. Absolutely not."

"All right then," Kat said. "Let's go sit down." She sat down at the kitchen table and took a sip of her wine. "It is good, isn't it?"

"Yes," Blaine said, but less than enthusiastically. "Tell us what's going on."

Kat told them about the conversation she'd had with Lennon, and how it had finally clicked in her mind that she was not only putting herself in danger unnecessarily, but the whole family.

"I don't see it that way," Lacie said. "You're noble. Lots of people have dangerous jobs. Like firefighters."

"But their families aren't in danger because of their work, are they, Lace?" Kat pointed out.

"Well, no, but… Fine. Detectives, then. Police officers in general. Their families could easily be targeted by criminals."

"But they have the resources to deal with that," Kat said. "I don't have any kind of protection at all, other than what Chief Moore is kind enough to provide when it's needed."

Lacie sighed, clearly out of ideas. "Come on, Blaine. Back me up. You're a lawyer, aren't you? Argue the case."

"I can't," Blaine said quietly. "Because I agree with Kat. I've thought the same thing for some time. I think as family members we're well enough protected, but I worry about Kat." He turned to her. "I really have been worried about you, far more than I've let on. I'm so glad it's finally over."

Kat winced. "Well, not quite. I have to finish what I started. I made a promise to Marion, and I'm not the kind of person to break promises. I'm going to complete this investigation and find out what really happened to her husband. Whether he died, or faked his own death, or had amnesia, or whatever."

Blaine nodded evenly. "All right. I can accept your desire to finish what you started."

"Now, here's the thing," Kat said. She took a large sip of her wine for courage. "We've gotten a new lead. Lennon's eldest son, Jethro, managed to get into Richard Molesey's email account and restored some deleted items. There were some plane tickets purchased. We're not sure if they were for a surprise trip for Marion, or if..."

"If he's faked his own death and fled the country," Lacie said.

"Exactly. I'm going to go there, to the destination, to see if I can track him down or find out anything. I'll need to be gone for about a week."

"So...?" Lacie looked at her expectantly.

"What?" Kat asked.

"Where is it?" Blaine pressed.

"Oh! Sorry," Kat said. "My head is everywhere right now. It's St. Lucia. An island in the Caribbean."

Lacie's mouth dropped open, then she began to smile. "Are you sure you want to finish all this investigating business, Mom? I mean a Caribbean vacation is a very nice tradeoff for being slightly exposed to a little bit of danger."

"Lacie," Kat said sternly. "Yes, I'm very serious about not doing any more investigating. It's too dangerous for my family. We can always take a Caribbean vacation without an investigation."

"True," Lacie said. "Anyway, I've decided I'm coming with you, with Florence."

"Absolutely not," Kat said. "It's too dangerous."

"It is not," Lacie said. "No one's been murdered. No one's been harmed. It's not a crazy killer on the loose that you're looking for."

"She's right about that," Blaine said.

"Look, I'm going back to work next week," Lacie said, "and I haven't taken a vacation in forever. This is the perfect opportunity. It seems almost meant to be."

"I don't know, Lacie," Kat said. "This is not making me feel very good. Say we go to a hotel, and I have to leave to do some investigative work. You and Florence will be on your own."

"Not if I come," Blaine said.

"What about your office?" Kat asked.

"We just cleared a huge backlog of cases," Blaine said, "so now's a relatively quiet time. My deputy Ryan can take over, and I can always work while I'm in St. Lucia. I haven't taken much vacation since Florence was born."

Kat sighed. "This was supposed to be a quick, investigative trip that allowed me to wrap up the case and hang up my amateur detective hat. Not a family vacation that might put you in danger."

"Aw, come on, Mom," Lacie said. "We want to support you."

"Agreed," Blaine said. "Especially since you've just told us that you won't be investigating again."

Kat smiled. "Well, all right. We'll book a wonderful all-inclusive hotel with plenty of things we can do with Lacie and Florence."

Lacie whooped. "Well, this is an unexpected treat."

"What the heck? The more the merrier," Kat said.

CHAPTER TWELVE

Kat's statement, "The more the merrier," turned out to be truer than they'd initially thought.

Not only did their party expand to Blaine, Lacie, and Florence, unfortunately Tyler couldn't get time off, but also to Mitzi and her husband Rex. Rex happened to have some vacation time, and he and Blaine had become good friends, so he decided to join them.

Mitzi was always game for a vacation, and managed to get her work in the acupuncture clinic scheduled in such a manner that she could take off for a few days and join them.

Lennon would have come, too, but a vacation for her was nothing short of a military operation that had to be planned at least a year in advance. She had too many responsibilities to attend to and simply couldn't get away.

Marion couldn't come, because she couldn't afford the cost of the trip. Blaine had offered to pay her family's way, but she'd acted embarrassed and declined. "Besides, we have to stay here for more tests for Betsy," she'd said, although Kat wasn't sure if that was just an excuse.

So a party of five adults and the baby flew out just two days after the discovery, thanks to Jethro's technical wizardry, that Richard had recently purchased airline tickets to St. Lucia.

"I think you could possibly be the best friend ever, Kat," Mitzi said, as they prepared to step off the plane into the heat of St. Lucia. "What a wonderful spur-of-the-moment decision."

"Are you sure?" Kat said. She wasn't quite feeling her sunny self since her revelation with Lennon. "It's not the best time of the year to come to the Caribbean. November, December, or perhaps January would have been better."

"My, my, my," Mitzi said, taking her sunglasses off the top of her head where they were resting against her topknot, and putting them on. "You know how people see a silver lining in a terrible situation. I think you're doing the opposite just now. That's not like you, Kat. Are you all right?"

Kat wasn't able to respond as they descended the stairs of the plane onto the tarmac, since the sound of a nearby plane was too loud, but when they got to the side of the runway and were walking through a shaded walkway, they were free to speak. Blaine and Rex were behind them, helping Lacie with all the baby paraphernalia she'd had to bring on the plane.

"Really, I'm not quite feeling myself," Kat told Mitzi. "Since I made the decision to stop investigating, I just wish it was all behind me. I've been putting my family and friends in danger, feeling guilty about it, and yet here you all are, right in the middle of my drama."

Mitzi put her arm around her briefly. "We're all adults who chose to be here. Well, apart from Florence, but Lacie made the decision to bring her along. You didn't urge us to come. You discouraged us, in fact. Very rudely, I might add."

She giggled and winked at Kat. "Just kidding. Anyway, the fact remains we are grown adults, and we're here of our own volition. You haven't dragged us into anything, so stop feeling guilty."

"Thanks," Kat said, although she still felt down.

Mitzi looked intensely at her. "What you need is a spa treatment or two, my dear. When we get to the hotel, promise me that's the first thing we'll do."

"All right," Kat said. "I booked a hair appointment and massage back in Lindsay, so it was on my radar."

"Good. At least you're starting to make some sense."

On the ride to the resort, Kat began to cheer up a little. How could she not? The scenery was simply breathtaking. St. Lucia was a beautiful lush island, with houses nestled into the vibrant green hillsides. The homes themselves were a colorful mix. Blue, and green, and yellow seemed to be very popular colors, with pastel shades mixed among them. Lacie pointed out a large house in a pleasing, if unconventional, shade of shocking pink.

They drove up the Caribbean Sea side of the island, the west coast. The driver had asked if they wanted to meander through scenic territory, stopping along the way for drinks and to take in the views, or if they'd prefer a shorter trip through the rugged and infinitely less beautiful east coast. They'd chosen the former option, and as Kat sat at a hilltop bar, with a view for miles and miles over the sea, she was glad they had.

The people were exceptionally friendly, and Lacie had a chance for a break with a cold beer, while a young woman who worked at the bar played a lively game of peek-a-boo with Florence. Thankfully they'd taken a night flight and bought Florence her own ticket, so she'd slept peacefully through the entire flight in her car seat. Now she was full of energy, bounding about and shrieking with laughter at the game.

Blaine, nursing his own cold beer, came over to where Kat was sitting. The bar had a back wall, two side walls, then was open in the front, meaning there was an absolutely beautiful view. A gentle breeze blew through the open air bar, which cooled the skin. Kat sat at the far end of the bar, as close to the view as she could get.

"Piton beer," Blaine said, nodding at his bottle. "Pitons view," he said, nodding at the two enormous mountains in front of them. St. Lucia was famous for them. They were truly magnificent.

"Yes," Kat said. "I was reading a plaque outside, and it said the people who lived here originally, the Arawaks I believe it said, thought the mountains had certain spiritual powers."

Blaine leaned on the railing and observed the Pitons again. "It's easy to see why, isn't it? They do inspire a certain awe."

"Yes, they do," Kat said.

After a moment of thought, Blaine said, "I think nature has tremendous powers over the human mind, or soul, whatever you'd like to call it. After spending time in nature, people almost always feel better. Less stressed."

"I agree," Kat said. "I wouldn't have phrased it quite that way, but it makes sense."

"I read an article online the other day," Blaine said, "about forest bathing, I think they call it. In Japan, medical insurance will pay for forest excursions to treat stress and various other mental health issues."

"Really? I've never heard of that," Kat said as she looked over the lush green landscape. "Perhaps I can do some forest bathing while we're here, to release some of my stress."

Blaine smiled and sat down next to her. He looked into her eyes and lowered his voice. "I don't want you to feel badly," he said. "You know I've been worried about you, but I don't want that to be a reason for you to feel guilty. I'm here to support you, not bring you down."

Kat smiled at him. "I know, but thank you for saying it. That helps. I'm just trying to get my head around going full steam on this investigation when my heart isn't in it anymore. I'm ready to move on."

"Like you said, you made a commitment to Marion."

"Yes," Kat said. "I may have made the commitment, but wanting to keep it is another matter. You know, to get up the energy to go ahead with it. I hadn't realized until now just how much mental energy it takes, doing all this."

"And physical energy," Blaine said. "Driving all over the place. Flying."

"Yes," Kat said, a little sadly. "It's like my eyes have finally been opened to how much of a toll it's been taking on all of us."

"Don't go down that road," Blaine said. "You've done some truly great things. You brought Marie's killer to justice, and the help you gave to Deborah and Luigi in Italy... well, they'll remember that all their life. You can be proud of all you've done, even while you're wrapping it up."

"That's true," Kat said. "I guess I'm just in a deep dark funk. I keep thinking I've been so stupid, and it was all a mistake."

"Not at all." Blaine said. He was so overcome with wanting to make her feel better, he put his arm around her. "You've done a wonderful service and helped a lot of people. I only hope life won't throw us so many curveballs in the future. I think you deserve some time to rest. And to enjoy Florence."

"Yes," Kat said. "Relaxing sounds like a wonderful idea, now that you mention it. I can focus on expanding my writing, and seeing my friends more often. And entertaining. I definitely want to do more entertaining." She was starting to feel better already.

"That's the spirit," Blaine said. "And there's the smile I love to see."

Kat couldn't keep from beaming. "You always know how to make everything all right, don't you?"

"You do the same for me," he said. "Pick me up when I'm down. If that's not what spouses are for, I don't know what they are."

Kat smiled. "I'm so lucky to have you."

Blaine took her hand and gently squeezed it.

After they left the bar and its gorgeous view, they drove on through winding, beautiful roads, and eventually arrived at the resort. The security gate had large earthen mounds on either side of it, bursting with colorful flowers.

"Oh, look at the anthurium," Mitzi, an avid gardener, said. She turned to her husband. "Rex, I think we should build a glass room onto the house. I could grow some exotic plants in it if we did."

"Interesting idea," Rex said. "Sounds expensive, but worth it."

Blaine laughed. "Good answer, Rex."

They went through the security gate, and drove up a large winding driveway to the resort, passing beautiful villas along the way. The villas were constructed to perfectly match the feel of the island painted in beautiful bright colors along with flowers, palms, and foliage growing all around them.

Lacie sighed with happiness. "As much as I love my work and our hometown, I think this is an ideal way to spend a Monday morning."

"I'll say," Mitzi said, laughing.

The driver drove them down a small hill to the reception area, where they checked in and met their hotel host, a friendly looking man called Eugene. He took them outside to a large golf cart and drove them up a hill, stopping in front of two beautiful villas, side by side, a larger one in a canary yellow, and a smaller one in lavender blue. Kat, Blaine, Lacie, and Florence were to take the larger one, while Mitzi and Rex would stay in the lavender blue villa.

"Thank you," Blaine said to the driver, after he'd helped unload all their bags. Eugene showed them all around the villas and told them about the different amenities that were available at the resort.

The canary yellow villa was absolutely beautiful inside. It had two bedrooms, and a large dining and seating area with an adjoining kitchen. Kat was glad they had a kitchen. She enjoyed eating out, but a kitchen would be handy to whip up something quickly if she needed to go out and investigate, and also if Florence needed something to eat.

The décor was light and breezy with white interior walls, pale blue shutters, and white linen drapes and upholstery. The effect was truly uplifting. The living area led onto a large terracotta patio area equipped with a large dining table and chairs, which was positioned so they would be in the shade.

The rest of the patio was open to the sun, complete with lounges, and a gorgeous swimming pool. It wasn't very large, actually more of a plunge pool, but it was tiled on the bottom and all around the sides with a mixture of purple, deep blue, and gold mosaic tiles. It was surrounded on two sides by a rock formation that trickled water down into the pool.

Kat loved the sound of running water, and she was so hot she felt like taking a dip in the pool immediately. In fact, it wasn't long before she could. As soon as Eugene left with a handsome tip in his pocket, Lacie said, "I'm going to take Florence in the pool."

"Good," Kat said. "I'll join you. I'm just going to book a couple of spa treatments for Mitzi and me. I think we'll go after lunch, so I'll have some time to spend in the pool with you."

It was a wonderful day, so full of new and pleasurable experiences that Kat forgot about everything that had been worrying her. She splashed around in the pool with Florence, who was absolutely elated and shrieked and splashed and flapped her arms, trying to swim.

A long lunch at the beach restaurant followed, where Kat had freshly caught snapper, wonderfully seasoned and grilled, with a huge salad and fries made from yams. Then she headed to the spa with Mitzi, where she had an aromatherapy massage designed for ultra-relaxation and a special body wrap using different herbs from the Caribbean region.

They didn't return from the spa until 5:00, and by then, all Kat had the strength for was to flop onto the bed and watch a movie. She couldn't even think about how to process the investigation or what she was going to do to get it moving. Blaine was out sailing with Rex, but came back shortly after Kat and joined her after taking a shower, similarly exhausted.

They decided to order a light dinner from room service, since they were far too tired to get dressed and go out to eat. Blaine ordered a seabass fillet in white wine sauce with salad and new potatoes, while Kat had stewed black eyed peas and jerk chicken with callaloo, a very Caribbean type of vegetable.

They ate dinner on the patio, while Lacie took Florence out for pizza, and toasted each other with white wine as they watched the sun set over the sparkling blue of the Caribbean.

It was the perfect end to a perfect day. Kat knew she'd have to start investigating as soon as the sun rose the next morning, but for now, all of that was forgotten. She was just enjoying the moment.

CHAPTER THIRTEEN

"It's absolutely scandalous," Michael Tomlinson said, pacing back and forth in the tiny lobby of the police station. It was so tiny that he could only pace for three or four steps before he had to turn and pace back again. He must have been back and forth at least a hundred times, despite Rebecca urging him to sit down.

Rebecca had given up trying to persuade him by then, and stoically sat in one of the uncomfortable metal chairs, biting her nails.

He looked at her with compassion and tenderness. "Don't worry, my love. I'm going to protect you. Whatever it takes."

"What if it takes moving to someplace other than this island?" she mumbled into her fingers. "Maybe this was all one big mistake."

He rushed over to her, knelt down in front of her and cupped her face in his hands. "Don't say that," he said. "Don't. Don't even think it. This is perfect. It's paradise." She didn't look convinced. "Believe it, Rebecca, my darling. All good things come with tests. This is our test. If we can make it through this, everything will be good. We'll get our perfect happily ever after, basking in the tropical sun. We will."

She looked up at him with weary eyes. "Do you promise?" she asked.

"I promise," he said firmly. "Don't worry. It's you and me against the world. And when you've got me on your side, you'll never have to fret again. I'm going to make everything okay."

She began to smile a little. "I know." She sighed. "I guess I was just getting worried. But you're my hero. My savior. I know you can make this work out."

"You bet I can." He went back to the empty front desk, and yelled "Hello? Is anyone here?" rather testily. They were at the police station to file a police report about the dead pig found on their doorstep. This 'Caribbean time' was charming most of the time, but when it came to official business, it was nothing short of infuriating.

There was no reply to his shouted inquiry.

"Good evening," someone said from behind them.

Michael spun around to see a short man with a camera around his neck. He had thick glasses and an unappealing smile. "Yes?" Michael said, immediately distrustful. He moved next to Rebecca protectively.

Without asking, the man lifted his camera and took a picture of the two of them. The camera flashed brightly, temporarily blinding Michael.

"Just what do you think you're doing?" Michael said, stepping up in front of the man.

The man stepped back abruptly, smiled and put out his hand for Michael to shake. "Eugene St. Clair of the Star newspaper," he said.

Michael didn't put out his own hand in return. "What do you want?"

"You're the couple who found the dead pig on your doorstep, right? I'm here to get all the details."

"No," Michael said. "We haven't even filed a report yet, and we'd prefer that our personal business not be splashed all over the island."

Eugene smiled. "You haven't been here very long, have you? Everybody knows everybody's business here. If your grandmother so much as coughs in the morning in her house in the north, everyone in the south will know about it by afternoon."

"Well, we'd prefer to be kept out of the island's gossip circle, thank you very much," Michael said.

"You can prefer anything you wish," Eugene said. "So far I know you're Americans, you had lunch at a local hotel, and late this afternoon you came back to your home and found a dead pig on your doorstep. Rumor has it it's because the land you've bought is family land and…"

"What's family land?" Rebecca asked.

"Land that was held in common between family members before land ownership was formalized with land papers," Eugene said. "The person you bought it from has their name on the deeds and there is no caution on it for any legal challenges of ownership, but I hear a few cousins from town have their grievances."

Michael was stunned into silence.

"How do you know all this?" Rebecca asked.

Eugene smiled proudly. "A good reporter makes it his business to know everything, by the method of efficient and penetrative research. I have already interviewed your neighbors."

He got out a pad of paper and raised his eyebrows. "Perhaps you would have been wise to do the same before you bought the property, since you would have found this information out before making a purchasing mistake."

"I'll not have you talk about my property purchases," Michael said tersely.

"It's a free country, sir," Eugene said. "Now, do you want to give me a first-hand account of what happened?"

"No," Michael said.

"Hello." It was a voice from the front desk area, where a policewoman had finally shown up.

Michael breathed a sigh of relief. "Thank goodness, it's about time."

He was about to ask her to remove the journalist, when the policewoman took off her police cap and rushed around the desk towards Eugene. She squealed with delight, squeezing him around the neck.

"If it isn't Eugene St. Clair," she said. "How have I been missing you for so long? It's been nearly a year. Where have you been hiding?"

"Oh," Eugene said, blushing and ducking his head, unable to stop smiling. "I've been here and there, picking up the best stories. I was off the island for a while too, in the U.S., doing some training courses. Keeping the pen sharp, you know."

"Well, it's just lovely to see you. How's your mother?"

"Doing well, doing well," Eugene said. "Still in the same house. She's enjoying her retirement."

"Fit and healthy?"

"Absolutely."

"Praise God," the policewoman said. "Be sure to say hello to her for me." She turned and looked at Michael and Rebecca. "What are you two doing here?"

Eugene nodded towards Michael and Rebecca, who by now

looked like they'd stepped into another world entirely and weren't quite sure what to make of it. "They found a dead pig on their doorstep."

The policewoman's eyes went wide with surprise. "Oh."

"Family land issue," Eugene said.

"Hmm, hmm, yes. Okay, well, don't trouble them, Eugene." She went back behind the desk and her demeanor changed almost instantly. She was suddenly very professional and serious, as if someone had flipped a switch. "Good evening, Sir, Madam," she said. "I hear you found a deceased animal on your property?"

"Yes," Michael said.

They began to file the report.

*****

Kat was also in a police station, a much larger and much more cheerful one. Lilting calypso music blared out of a radio, and a lady with a basket came around selling colorful fresh local juices in bottles along with bags of various little fruits to the people in line at the station. Kat bought a tamarind juice to take back to Lacie. It was her favorite, and they didn't have it at the hotel.

The line was long, and the police at the desk were doing nothing to speed it up. She looked ahead and saw them listen attentively to each person, and then fill out paperwork. It was rather tiresome, especially as the elderly woman in front of her launched into a long soliloquy about her stolen goat, which then turned out to be her analysis of the characters that lived in her neighborhood, theorizing who could have done it.

Or was it someone from out of town? She had numerous, numerous theories, and the young policeman at the desk was clearly far too polite to interrupt. He had large, innocent eyes and was a handsome young man, who looked like he was barely out of high school. Kat wasn't sure how on earth he'd manage to stand up to hardened criminals.

But when it was her turn, she was glad for his gentleness and the patient manner in the way in which he dealt with people's problems.

"Good morning, ma'am. I'm Officer Charlery," he said. "How can I help you?"

"Hi there, good morning, Officer Charlery," Kat said. "I'm looking for someone. I'm wondering if you might have some information on him, or know where he might be?"

"Sure," Officer Charlery said. "Do you have any identification for the person?"

"Yes," Kat said. "I have his passport." She took it out of her purse and handed it to him.

He flipped it to the photo page. "Okay. Richard Molesey."

"Yes."

"Is he your husband?"

"No," Kat said. "My friend's husband."

"Are you on vacation?"

"Well… yes, I suppose," she said. "Not with my friend, though."

He looked up at her, clearly bemused, looking for an explanation.

Kat smiled. "It's a little complicated."

"I'm not in a rush," he said, despite the line stretching to the front door. "Go ahead."

Kat explained what was going on and why she was there, ending with, "And I've started trying to track him down today."

"I see," he said. "Would you like to file a missing persons report?"

"Not really," Kat said. "I'd just like to see if you have a record of him anywhere, or anything like that. Or if you could help me with getting information from banks or the driver's registration department, you know, places like that."

"You can only get that information if you open a missing persons report," he said. "And it wouldn't be you doing the asking, it would be us. And we would not open the missing persons report until he has been missing two weeks on-island, and you would have to have proof that at some point he was on the island. And then after another month we would do a cursory check around banks, hotels, hospitals and the like."

Kat wasn't impressed. "You're telling me that there wouldn't be any action for six weeks?"

"Yes, ma'am."

"I'll be back in Kansas by then."

"Oh, you live in Kansas? I have cousins in Kansas City. I hope to go there next year."

"You should, it's lovely," Kat said. "But can't you do something more quickly on Richard Molesey?"

"Let me search the system first," he said. "And then the filing cabinet."

"Please."

He typed the name into his computer and grimaced. "Nothing, I'm afraid, ma'am. I can check the filing cabinet, too, though I'm not holding out any hope."

"Thank you."

"You can go and sit down in the waiting area."

He went into a back room and Kat went to sit down. She took out her phone and saw a text from Blaine, *any luck?*

She replied, *not so far.*

She was shocked and disheartened to see the time on her phone. It was nearly 11:00 a.m. She'd arrived at the police station just after 9:00. She knew she'd been waiting a long time, but didn't realize it had been that long. Evidently the interesting people watching she'd done while she was waiting in line had made the time go a little faster than she'd thought.

It wasn't too long before Officer Charlery came back. He had a folder in his hand, and she rushed over, feeling her hopes picking up.

"I'm afraid there's nothing, ma'am," he said, sliding the folder over to the officer who was sitting next to him. It was a folder about something else entirely.

"Oh," Kat said, feeling deflated. "What do you suggest I do next?"

"You can open a missing persons report," he said. "It's your call."

"That's not going to work," Kat said. "I need something more immediate."

"I'm really sorry," he said, and his big eyes did look like he sincerely meant it. "I wish you the best of luck. Is there anything else I can help you with?"

"No," Kat said. "Thanks for trying, Officer Charlery."

Kat stepped out of the air-conditioned police station into the blazing hot sun. She flipped her shades down off her hair and over her eyes and sighed deeply. All that waiting she'd done had been for nothing.

The saving grace to the morning was that the police station was directly opposite the beach, and it was a lovely day. The perfect blue waves lapping up and down on the sandy shore looked inviting, as did the beach bar with a huge sweeping veranda overlooking the Caribbean Sea.

"I need to regroup and get my thoughts together," Kat said to herself, crossing the street. She looked at the drink menu and then ordered a pina colada with plenty of ice.

She sipped it at a table at the far edge of the veranda, the gentle sound of the waves providing a soundtrack to her snatched moment of relaxation.

Well, she thought. *It's not the worst place in the world I could be failing in an investigation.*

CHAPTER FOURTEEN

After her brief stop at the beachside bar, Kat spent a very hot and frustrating afternoon going all over town, the name Richard Molesey ringing in her ears, as she went from bank to bank, hotel to hotel. She waited in long lines, managed to skip other long lines, got taxi rides here and there, and tried to be as persuasive as possible, but all to no avail.

About three visits into her traipsing around, she started to pretend Richard was her missing husband. Otherwise everyone asked for the full story, which was long and complicated. She didn't like to lie, but she saw it as being an economical way to deal with her time constraints as well as being not too far from the truth.

By the time she was in a cab on her way back to the resort, she was totally and utterly frazzled. Her flip flops had rubbed the part between her big toe and the next toe completely raw on both feet, so that it hurt to walk, and she had to hobble around. Her hair was a frizzy mess. She was completely overheated and sticky and wanted nothing more than to jump into a bath of ice cubes.

Even the walk from the cab to the shuttle to take her up the hill to their villa felt insurmountable. Thankfully it was only 5:00 p.m., so she'd have plenty of time to rest before dinner. She'd encouraged Mitzi to stay at the resort and enjoy herself. She'd wanted to join Kat, but Kat absolutely refused.

"You're always so busy at the clinic," she'd said, "you deserve a break." It had taken quite some persuading, because Mitzi was a very good arguer. But Kat refused to let her ruin her vacation by helping her with the investigation. "Maybe tomorrow," she'd said as they ended their conversation.

When she got back to the villa, she found Lacie and Florence taking a quick afternoon dip.

"How did it go, Mom?" Lacie asked, bouncing Florence up and down in the water.

Kat smiled at them both and gave Florence a tired little wave. "Not that fantastically," Kat said.

"Any leads?"

"Nada."

Lacie gave her a sympathetic grimace. "Perhaps tomorrow."

"Let's hope," Kat said. "Right now all I want is a nice cold shower. It was hot everywhere I went."

"I can imagine," Lacie said. "It was so hot at the beach we had to come back here."

Kat barely had the energy to reply. "See you in a little while," she said, as she went inside.

She found Blaine sitting in one of the armchairs in the bedroom with a cold beer, reading a book. His forehead was very red as he looked up at her. "Hello, darling," he said.

"Hello," she said. "You've definitely been in the sun. You're red."

His eyes widened. "I doubt if I'm as red as you are."

"Really?" She walked over to the mirror and looked at herself.

"Help! I look like a lobster."

He chuckled. "Well, at least you're a very pretty lobster."

Kat flopped down on the bed.

"I know that look," Blaine said. "I take it you had a disappointing day?"

"Yes." Kat sighed as she stared up at the ceiling. "A complete and utter waste of time. I got precisely zilch."

"Sorry to hear that," Blaine said. He came over and sat down next to her. "You look like you need a massage."

"Isn't the spa closed at this time?"

"Yes," he said. "I meant I could give you one."

"Oh, that sounds like heaven," Kat said. "But first, I need the sweet paradise of a cold shower."

Blaine smiled. "Try not to think too much about the investigating. It can wait until tomorrow."

"That seems like a good idea," Kat said. "I think my mind needs a break."

Kat went into the bathroom and took a gloriously refreshing cold shower. It was, she thought, the most satisfying shower she'd ever had in her entire life. After she'd dried off, she laid down on the bed, and Blaine turned himself into a masseur.

"You're rather good at this," Kat said. "I'll have to commission your services more often when we get back to Kansas."

"Fine with me," he said. "We need to make more time for things like this. There are other things I'd like to make time for too, like dancing, and going out for an evening. I never think of them until we go on vacation."

Kat sighed. "You're right. When we get away, we do all those magical things. But at home, they sort of slip off our radar, don't they?"

"Yes. Let's make a concerted effort when we get back. Maybe we should even schedule them in our calendars while we're still here. I'd like to take you to that jazz bar we went to a few times," he said. "Do you remember how much fun we had? Getting dressed in our best, dancing the night away to jazz."

Kat sighed with happiness. "It was great, wasn't it? Let's definitely go there again."

"Yes, we absolutely have to do that when we get back."

"That's the thing with being self-employed," Kat said. "It's wonderful, because you don't have a schedule. But that's also the reason it's not wonderful. It starts to encroach on Saturday nights, and before you know it, all you think about is work. I do love my writing, but sometimes I think I need to have more set hours to do it in."

"That might help."

"But then, I want the flexibility to be able to take off for a hair appointment, or do something with Florence, or come and have an impromptu lunch with you. It's a double-edged sword, I suppose. Comes with both benefits and drawbacks."

"Yes," Blaine said. "I often feel the same about my job as District Attorney. Even though I have set hours, the buck stops with me. That means I have to do whatever it takes, however long it takes, to make sure everything is in order. I can't just clock out at 5:00 p.m."

"I know," Kat said. "You often work into the night long after dinner, don't you?"

Blaine smiled. "So do you. It's quite companionable."

"Yes, I suppose it is." She paused. "When do you think you'll retire?"

"That's the million-dollar question," he said. "I don't know, Kat. There are times I resent the workload, in busy periods, and wish I was free to spend hours doing whatever I wanted to. But I think I'd enjoy that for about six months, maybe a year. Then I think I'd be chomping at the bit for something to do."

"Hmm, yes, I can't see you sitting around the house much."

"No. We could travel more, though."

"That would be nice."

"What about you?" he asked. "Retirement, I mean?"

"Well, I'm very much enjoying my writing," she said. "I may get to the position where my back catalogue is enough to see me through, but I think I'd miss creating new stories and releasing them. It's enjoyable. I can see myself doing it for years and years to come."

"I'm glad you enjoy your work," he said. "That makes life a lot easier."

"It does," she agreed. "You make life a lot easier, too."

"I do?"

"You know you do," she said with a laugh. "Stop fishing for compliments."

After her massage, Kat fell asleep and by the time she woke up, it was dark outside. She sat bolt upright, scrambling for her phone to see what time it was and wondering if she'd slept through dinner.

But before she could reach it, Blaine came ambling in from the bathroom, applying cologne. "We decided to make it a late dinner, given how tired you were," he said. "We got the latest reservation available, 9:30."

"Thanks," Kat said. "I really appreciate that."

"I let you sleep as long as possible," Blaine said with a grin. "I just called you from the bathroom. I take it that's why you woke up?"

Kat still felt a little groggy. "I guess. How long do I have?"

"Fifteen minutes."

"I can work with that," she said.

"You could go down to dinner looking like that," he said. "You're naturally beautiful."

Kat laughed, swinging her legs out of bed. "With this bird's nest on my head? You're kind, Blaine, but rather ridiculous."

He chuckled. "That's the thanks I get for making a compliment around here."

Kat laughed along with him. "Try to make it more believable next time." She put on a deep pink dress that highlighted her coloring and always brought her compliments. She wore muted jewelry to accompany it. It was an understated yet elegant look.

She didn't have enough time to wash her hair and blow dry it, so she worked with what she had, the half wave, half curl her hair took to naturally, and put it into an artfully dishevelled updo. She slipped her feet into some simple brown high heels. With rose quartz dangly earrings, her outfit was complete.

"Wow, you look spectacular," Mitzi said as they met outside the villas to walk down to the restaurant. Lacie had opted to stay home with Florence and had already eaten dinner, compliments of room service.

"Thank you," Kat said. "So do you!"

Mitzi really did, with a figure-hugging dress in a lovely shade of periwinkle blue. Rex and Blaine took off towards the restaurant, and Kat and Mitzi hung back, walking a little slower, enjoying the evening.

"So?" Mitzi asked.

"Not a trace of him," Kat answered.

"Oh dear." Mitzi patted her on the arm comfortingly. "But there's always tomorrow. And tomorrow, I'm coming with you, whether you like it or not."

"You're so insistent, I think it would be rude for me to say no again," Kat said. "As long as you're sure I'm not ruining your vacation."

"Not at all," Mitzi said. "I'd like to help."

"Well, all right then," Kat said.

Kat had been feeling tired, but when they reached the restaurant and soaked in the ambience of the tropical evening, she was instantly revived. They drank fine white wine and ate wonderful fresh seafood. Kat had grilled dorado, which was simply divine, followed by a fresh fruit plate.

They ended up staying out until nearly midnight, talking and laughing, and enjoying the view of the gently rippling sea in the moonlight. Kat loved how the lights on the pier and the light of the moon danced like diamonds on the surface of the water, here one moment, gone the next.

On the way back to their villas, they were all rather giggly and very happy indeed.

"I think I'll sleep in tomorrow morning and have a late breakfast,"

Kat said. "Then we'll be ready to go investigating, Mitzi."

Mitzi gave her a wobbly salute. "Aye, aye, Cap'n Kat." Then she nearly fell over on Rex.

Rex looked at her and laughed. "I think sleeping in tomorrow morning is going to be a necessity for you as well, Mitzi," he said. "And as a doctor, I think an aspirin or two might not be a bad idea."

Blaine laughed and said, "Goodnight."

The next morning went as planned, for the most part. They each slept in, Mitzi had her aspirin, and they had a late breakfast at the resort restaurant. Kat played with Florence for a few minutes, then she and Mitzi got up from the patio area by the large pool, ready to leave.

"Wait," Blaine said. "I think… I think your investigation might just be over."

CHAPTER FIFTEEN

"What do you mean the investigation might be over?" Kat asked, pushing her sunglasses on top of her head and looking down at Blaine.

He sat up in his lounger. "You showed me a picture of Richard before we left. Is it me, or does this look a lot like him?" He showed Kat the newspaper he was reading.

Kat looked at the picture. It was a little blurry, but it definitely looked like Richard Molesey. "I think it's him," she said, her heart beating faster.

Mitzi, Rex, and Lacie, with Florence on her hip, rushed behind Kat to look over her shoulder at the picture.

"Definitely!" Lacie cried out. "That's got to be him."

"I wonder who the woman is," Mitzi said, pointing to the woman sitting down in a metal chair in front of Richard.

Kat read the headline. "*American Couple Finds Dead Pig On Their Doorstep Over Family Land Feud.* Goodness me."

Lacie continued. "Michael Tomlinson and his fiancée Rebecca Norman were shocked and sickened to discover..."

"So Michael Tomlinson's his fake name," Mitzi said. "And it looks like he faked his own death to start a new life in the Caribbean with this Rebecca woman."

"If that's even her real name," Lacie said. She shook her head. "People like him make me sick. He has four kids, for Pete's sake!"

"One of which is a very sick kid, to boot," Kat added. Her head was racing. "Where did this come from? I want to go and find out about this article."

"Dominica," Rex said. "Look." He pointed at the article.

"I think that's the next island over," Kat said. "I wonder how we can get there."

Blaine took out his phone. "Let me check."

Kat continued to examine the article while Blaine was looking it up. "What I don't understand is why they'd let themselves be photographed and have the story in the paper if they've changed their identities. Surely it'd be too risky?"

"That's true," Lacie said. "Maybe they think because they're on a remote island no one they know will ever find out about it?"

"Maybe," Kat said. "Still, it seems pretty shortsighted. I know if I changed my identity, I'd want to keep away from anything like having my name and photograph appear in a local newspaper."

"Me too," Mitzi said. She elbowed Rex in the ribs. "You and Blaine had better watch out, honey. Kat and I might change our identities and come out to the islands for a permanent girls' holiday. Oh, and Lacie and Florence, too."

Kat was too perplexed to appreciate Mitzi's kidding around. "Wait a minute," she said, scanning down the article. "There are actually no quotes from the couple at all. They're mostly from neighbors. It says this photo was taken in the police station, and I think they look like it caught them off guard. Maybe it was taken without their permission, and they didn't have any input into the article at all."

"That's a good point," Rex said. "I don't see any quotes from them either. It doesn't say where they come from in the U.S., either. It just says they're American. Surely if they'd contributed something to the article, it would say exactly where they were from and what they were doing on the island."

"I think you're absolutely right," Kat said.

"Ah," Blaine said, looking up from his phone. "Kat, it's no problem for us to get to Dominica. And you're right, it's the next island over. All we have to do is take a ferry. It will take us about a half hour to get to the ferry to take us there.

"Taking a plane won't work because there's only one flight a week and it will be several days before the next flight leaves."

"Sounds good to me," Kat said.

"It seems like fate is smiling on us," Blaine said, "because the ferry only goes there twice a week, and one is going there today."

"Great," Kat said. "I really want to get this wrapped up now. Poor Marion."

"There's one small problem," Blaine said.

Kat looked at him quizzically.

"The ferry leaves in one hour."

"Help!" Kat shouted as she jumped up from the chair where she'd been sitting.

They sprang into action, all of them rushing to the reception area, where they took a shuttle up to the villas. Thankfully there was an empty one waiting. Blaine quickly spoke to the reception desk before they left, saying they needed a taxi immediately and have it sent to their villa.

On the way to their villa, they decided that Kat and Blaine would go alone to Dominica, while Mitzi, Rex, Lacie, and Florence would stay at the resort. Otherwise, it would just be too complicated.

Kat volunteered to go to Dominica alone, but Blaine wouldn't hear of it. "You never know, this Richard character could be dangerous."

"I don't think so," Kat replied. "He certainly didn't give off a hint of violence in any of the family things Marion showed me."

"He's a totally unknown quantity, Kat," Blaine said. "If he can fake his own death and have his wife and children mourn him while he's sunning himself in the Caribbean with a new woman, I wouldn't put anything past him."

"Blaine has a point, Kat," Mitzi said.

As soon as the shuttle was at the top of the hill, they rushed into the villa. "You get the passports and documents and money and all of that," Kat said to Blaine. "I'll pack our things."

"I'll help," Mitzi said.

Kat began rushing around like a madwoman trying to get everything packed as quickly as possible. She tossed clothing from the closet right into a travel bag without folding any of it, which was totally unlike her.

Mitzi went into the bathroom and grabbed their toothbrushes, toothpaste, and a hair brush. "Don't forget what people always forget when they're in a hurry," she said. "Your phone chargers."

"Good point," Kat said. "And I would have forgotten them. They're on our nightstands." Her eyes looked over at them. "Would you put Blaine's watch in the front pocket of our bag?"

A couple of minutes later they were packed and ready to go. Kat barely had time to hug Mitzi, Lacie, and little Florence.

"Grandma and Grandpa are going on a quick trip, Florence, darling," she said. She gave her a kiss on each squishy cheek, then on the forehead. "See you soon. Have a great time while we're gone. We'll be back soon."

Lacie gave Kat another hug at the door as they left. "Go catch that awful man," she said.

"We'll certainly try," Kat said. "See you, everyone."

There was no time for any long goodbyes. Kat and Blaine got into the cab, and Blaine immediately explained their situation and how much of a rush they were in to the driver, who introduced himself as Kennedy.

Kennedy smiled at them through the rearview mirror. "I want to tell you a fascinating fact about St. Lucia."

Kat didn't feel it was quite the time, but politely said, "Please do."

"St. Lucia has no speed limit."

Kat and Blaine laughed.

"Well, go ahead and step on it, Kennedy," Blaine said.

"I'll be glad to, as soon as we get out of the resort complex," Kennedy replied. "I don't want to lose my contract with the hotel."

"Yes, of course," Kat said.

As they drove, Blaine and Kat both had their eyes locked onto the digital clock on Kennedy's dashboard. They made good time along the highway, but after about twenty minutes found themselves stuck in slow traffic.

"There's a chance they'll close the passenger gate late," Kennedy said. "They often do that. Even if you get there after they close it, it still takes time to get everything started on the ferry and get out to sea. They could let you on then, as a late arrival."

"Let's hope so." Kat was glad for Kennedy's optimism, but she couldn't help but feel he might be wrong.

The clock was ticking down, and soon there were only three minutes to go until the gate would close.

"We're not going to make it, Kennedy, are we?" Blaine asked.

Kennedy didn't answer. He made a hard right turn out of the backroad they were on, went over a cross street, made a left, and then came out in an area that looked like they were in the middle of nowhere, but they were facing the docks.

"Oh, we're here!" Kat said.

"Yes," Kennedy replied. "Just a moment, because we have to drive through security, but then I will take you right up to the passenger gate."

"Great," Blaine said.

It took only a moment to go through security, the officer waving them through, and then the ferry gate was right in front of them. Kat peered through the windshield and saw a young family walking through it. Then a woman in uniform looked around, didn't see anyone else, and closed the gate.

Kennedy slammed on the handbrake and jumped out of the car. "Miss!" he shouted. "I have two passengers here for you!"

"Okay," she said, re-opening the gate.

Kat sighed with relief as she and Blaine hurried out of the car. Kennedy got their single travel bag from the back, and they rushed to the gate. Kat had already paid Kennedy, but Blaine gave him a handsome tip. "Thank goodness for the lack of speed limit, huh?" Blaine said with a grin.

Kennedy nodded. "Thanks, sir. Have a great trip, both of you."

"We will," Kat said. "Thank you again, Kennedy."

Everything went smoothly as they boarded the ferry. The ship was no luxurious cruise liner, but it was clean, comfortable, and did the job. There was a bar and a quaint little Caribbean restaurant on the ship. Kat had eaten a large late breakfast, and it was only noon, so she didn't have an appetite yet, but the food smelled so good she decided to buy some and take it with them.

They each got a cold beer and settled down in the lounge.

"Have you had a chance to book a hotel?" Kat asked. "I'll be very impressed if you did, since we barely had a spare second, and that cab ride was so suspenseful."

"I didn't," he said. "Would you like me to?"

"Sure, or I will. I don't mind," she said. "If we could check in, dump our travel bag, and begin our search, that would be great."

"Yes," Blaine said. "You know, this is the first time I've ever really been involved in one of your investigations. I know this sounds a little crude, but it is pretty… fun, isn't it? Exciting, in a way."

Kat grinned. "Aha! You've caught the investigating bug, Mr. Evans. We agreed this was to be my last case. Do I sense a change of heart on your part? Is a husband and wife private investigator firm playing on your brain?"

Blaine smiled. "No. I expect it sounds more fun than it actually would be. We'd probably get a lot of paranoid husbands spying on their wives to find out if they're cheating."

"Oh, that can't be all of it," Kat said. "You could decide which cases you'd take, not that I'm advocating it for a moment. As exciting as the prospect would be, I've already said I want to give myself a little break and focus on writing."

"You could write a series about it," Blaine suggested. "A husband and wife duo. He has the legal know-how from being a DA, and she has the investigator's genius from writing so many murder mysteries. They set up with a third partner, perhaps his brother who's a retired cop, but on the day they open for business, they find him dead, and that's the first case they have to investigate."

Kat laughed. "Goodness, Blaine. Looks like I should employ you to plot out some storylines for me."

Blaine laughed along with her, then looked at her quite seriously, his eyes full of love. "As glad as I am about you letting this go, I have to say, I think you're remarkable. I mean, who could have imagined I'd be here, right now, doing what I'm doing, with a wonderful woman like you?"

Kat smiled. "Thanks, honey. You sure I'm not ruining your island vacation?"

"You're the reason I'm on this island vacation," he said, rolling his eyes at her. "That was partly my point."

"Oh, I see. Well…"

But Kat didn't get the time to reply, because a grey and white pitbull, coming out of nowhere, jumped up on her. She was a dog lover through and through, but it was such a shock, she screamed.

CHAPTER SIXTEEN

"Darla!" a man yelled as he rushed over and pulled the pitbull off of Kat. "Ma'am, I am so, so sorry." He turned to a girl next to him who had a headful of braids with click-clacking beads woven through them, who must have been about seven. They resembled one another, so Kat assumed he was her father. "Darla, I told you not to let go of the leash!"

"Sorry, Dad. He yanked it out of my hand." Darla put her head down and acted contrite.

Kat felt sorry for her, now that she'd recovered from the shock. "It's okay, honest. I'm all right. I love dogs. I have two at home myself."

The man smiled. "Me, too. I've got six at home. I have a dog sitter who takes care of them when I'm away, but this guy..." He looked down at the dog he was now holding on a short leash, who was looking up at him, suddenly very docile. Kat got the impression the man was a bit of a dog whisperer.

"Well, Sammy is new to my little pack, and my dog sitter doesn't feel comfortable with him yet. He's boisterous. Not aggressive, just very excitable. He thinks he's still a puppy."

Kat chuckled. "He is cute."

"Maybe," the man said with a laugh. "Anyway, I really am sorry he jumped up on you like that. May I buy you a drink?"

"You don't need to," Kat said.

"Oh, go on, sir," the man said to Blaine. "Persuade her for me, or I'll feel guilty the whole ride back. Why don't I get a beer for you, too?"

Blaine and Kat smiled at each other.

"Well, all right then, if you insist," Blaine said.

The man went to the bar, positioning Sammy at his heels and holding him on a short tight leash. They could see him talking sternly to Darla.

"I think she's getting a little lecture," Kat said.

"Rightly so," Blaine said. "They're very lucky it was you the dog jumped on, rather than anyone else. Someone else would have gone crazy, and might even be feeling litigious."

"That's true," Kat said. "But it was just an honest mistake."

"Thankfully with a happy ending."

In a few moments, the man returned with Sammy at his heels. He was carrying two beers, while Darla carried another beer and a soda. They sat at the table next to Kat and Blaine, which was close enough for them to chat comfortably.

"Thank you," Kat said as the man set the beers down in front of them.

"Cheers," Blaine said, holding up his bottle. "To our journey to Dominica." Everyone touched his bottle, even Darla, though she looked a little shy about it. "What takes you to Dominica, then... Sorry, I don't know your name. I'm Blaine and this is my wife, Kat."

Kat smiled. "This pretty girl is Darla. The boisterous dog is Sammy. So who is the generous man?"

"Embarrassed, more than generous," he said with a chuckle. "I'm Kelvin. I'm headed back to Dominica to take Darla back to her mother. I'm Dominican by birth, but I live in St. Lucia now for work. Darla comes to see me every month for a week. I'll stay a couple days in Dominica and then take the ferry back."

"You get to go on a ferry every month?" Kat said to Darla. "That's kind of exciting, isn't it?"

Darla cuddled into her father, the shyness of a seven-year-old, apparent.

"Answer the lady," Kelvin prompted gently.

"Yes, ma'am," Darla said.

"Aww," Kat said, looking at Blaine.

"What are you guys doing?" Kelvin asked. "Are you on vacation?"

Kat looked at Blaine again.

"Of sorts," he answered.

"Honeymoon?" Kelvin asked.

"No," Kat said. Normally she wouldn't be so open with a stranger, but Kelvin's manner put her at ease. He seemed like a nice, easy-going guy. Still, she wasn't going to tell him the whole truth. "We're doing some research. I'm a writer."

Neither of those things was a lie, she reasoned with herself. The facts were just not quite as connected as they appeared.

"Oh, nice!" he said. "Are you setting a book in Dominica?"

"I'm considering it," she replied.

"Well, I could show you around, if you'd like," he said.

"Would you?" Kat said. "That would be wonderful!"

"Anywhere you're going in particular?"

"It's a little village called Martine," Blaine said, referencing the newspaper article.

"Ah, yes, I know the place," Kelvin said. "Nice, actually. I was thinking of picking up some real estate there, so I wouldn't mind going myself."

"Well, that works out perfectly, then," Kat said. "It sounds just right for us. Thank you."

They chatted the rest of the way about all sorts of things. They discussed Kat and Blaine's work at length, since Kelvin was fascinated by what they did. He was a tax accountant, so really there wasn't much to discuss except how income tax rates differed in the islands as compared to Kansas.

But he had a wide range of interests, and they touched on bird watching, bare-hand river fishing, the best ways to cook seafood, cricket, and once they hit on travel, there was no stopping them. He told them about his plans to take Darla to Japan. They'd already done Dubai and Paris, and Kat and Blaine spoke about their dream destinations, too.

The conversation was so fascinating that the ferry ride seemed too short. As the ferry pulled into Roseau, the main town on Dominica, Kat realized they hadn't made a hotel reservation, so she made a few calls. Thankfully, there had been a last-minute cancellation at a nice hotel just outside of town. Kelvin had recommended it.

"I can come meet you tomorrow morning there," he said, "and we'll head to Martine."

"Thanks," Blaine said, shaking his hand. "Great to have met you, Kelvin."

"Likewise. If it's okay with you, I'll pick you up in the morning at your hotel at 10:00 a.m."

They all said goodbye, and Darla surprised Kat by running up to her for a quick hug.

Once they'd disembarked, they got a cab to take them to their hotel. The whole way, Blaine talked about Kelvin. "Great guy, great guy," he kept saying. Kat hadn't seen him so enthused about anyone for a long time, so it was nice to see that he'd found someone he liked.

The hotel was small, intimate, and right on the beach. It seemed to be popular with couples, and the staff was very kind and accommodating. Kat and Blaine made a dinner reservation and then took a walk on the beach. There were people offering sailboat rides, and since it was only 4:00 p.m., and they had plenty of time before dinner, they decided to go on one.

Their boat guide was an elderly Rastafarian man with long gray dreadlocks. He didn't speak much, just looked out over the water, and Kat was glad he had little to say. It made the moment ever more special, almost reverent. He seemed to totally blend in with everything, as if he was part of nature.

Kat and Blaine sat near the front of the boat, looking out over the turquoise water that seemed to stretch out forever.

Kat sighed with happiness. "Life is strange, isn't it, darling?"

"How do you mean?"

"Pardon the philosophical mindset, only the juxtaposition of this boat ride and the investigation into this clearly sordid man, makes me think..."

"Of what?"

"How lucky we are, really. Do you think that could be another reason why I choose to investigate these tragedies all the time?"

"I'm not following you, Kat," Blaine said. "What do you mean?"

"I wonder if…" Kat paused and looked out over the sea. "I wonder if I feel guilty for being so happy. You know, for everything in our life going so smoothly."

"Hmm… Maybe. But why would it make you feel guilty?"

"It's just that everyone in the world has troubles, and without meaning to sound smug, maybe we're not getting our fair share of those troubles. I'm not wishing anything bad for us, but…"

"I don't think it's even true," Blaine said. "You lost your first husband in a car accident, Kat. When that happened, it caused a lot of trouble in your life."

"I know," Kat said. "Since then, I mean. Or maybe it's even connected to that. Maybe I feel guilty about being so happy, so I'm investigating these different cases out of guilt." She laughed darkly. "As some kind of service to my husband's fellow dead."

"I think that's a bunch of bull," Blaine said. "I don't think that's true at all. I think you simply have a kind heart, an investigative mind, and a strong thirst for justice, and that combination makes these mysteries irresistible to you."

"Hmm. That's interesting, because that's the way I would have described you."

"Maybe that's why we get along so well," Blaine said. "We're on the same wavelength. Those are attributes I need in my work. I've also often thought you'd be very good at my job."

"Have you? Do you think so?"

"Absolutely stellar."

"Hmm. Well, that's a nice compliment. Thanks. If I was twenty years younger, I might just retrain." She laughed. "So let me see... a kind heart, an investigative mind, and a strong thirst for justice. Now I need to figure out how I can get all of those needs met without becoming a female Inspector Poirot every five minutes."

"A slim, attractive female Poirot."

"That's not much better," Kat said with a laugh. "Well, the kind heart part... I can look after Florence. The investigative mind I can apply to my books, and put my characters in all kinds of investigating shenanigans. A strong thirst for justice is trickier."

"You could always volunteer somewhere," Blaine suggested. "I'm sure there are lots of causes you could get behind and support."

"That's true," Kat said. "That's certainly something to think about. Well, I do apologize for my excessive navel-gazing, Blaine, but it has helped."

"Not necessary at all," Blaine said. "When you need to process, I'm here to talk it through. Always."

"Love you," Kat said. She leaned over and kissed him on the cheek.

"Love you, too."

When they returned, they had a nice dinner in the hotel restaurant, which overlooked the sea. It wasn't the sumptuous Creole fare the St. Lucian resort restaurant had served, because it was obviously catered toward tourists with slightly less adventurous tastes. Still, Kat had a perfectly nice chicken burger, yam fries, and a salad, while Blaine had fried fish, a salad and battered onion rings. They both had ice cream for dessert.

"Simple but effective," Blaine said once they were finished with dinner.

"Yes," Kat agreed. "It won't win any Michelin stars, but it was just fine."

Their room was the same, nothing spectacular, but it was clean, comfortable, and nicely decorated. It did the job, and that's all they needed. Although the room was small, they had a nice little balcony overlooking the sea, so they stayed up with a glass of wine, watching the reflection of the moon dance on the waves. They checked up on Lacie, Florence, Mitzi, and Rex, who were all fine. Kat managed to do some work on her mystery book, and Blaine caught up on some of his work, as well.

After a restful sleep, they woke up early and had a breakfast of fresh fruit and pastries. There was just time for a quick walk on the beach before Kelvin came to meet them.

He pulled up in a very nice silver Mercedes promptly at 10:00 a.m.

"Morning, Kelvin," Kat said. "Looks like we're traveling in style to Martine."

"Indeed," Kelvin replied. "I always like to pick up a nice rental car when I'm over here."

Blaine and Kelvin said good morning to each other. Kat got in the back seat next to Sammy, who was asleep, and she insisted that Blaine ride up front. She didn't want Kelvin to feel he was their taxi driver.

Once they got out of town it was a very nice scenic ride to Martine.

"Martine is quite deep inside the island," Kelvin said. "But it's very high up, so it has excellent views. It's very scenic, which is why it seems to be taking off for real estate investors. Well, that and the low land prices."

"Are you looking to buy as an investor?" Blaine asked. "Or to build, or…?"

"I think I should really have a house here on Dominica," Kelvin said. "When I was with Darla's mother, Sophia, we owned a family home, but when we divorced, I insisted she keep it, especially since I was going to be in St. Lucia for work.

"I built my home in St. Lucia, but I think having a second home here would be good, too. When I have any vacation from work, I come here to spend time with Darla, if we're not traveling, and I always stay in hotels and guesthouses. I think it would be better for me to have a permanent home on the island."

"That's probably a good idea," Kat said. "Who would look after it for you while you're away?"

"I'm considering building a four-plex," he said. "I could rent out the other units, and then I can just lock up and leave when I feel like it. Plus, I'd get some passive income."

"Sounds like a win-win situation to me," Blaine said.

"That's what I'm hoping," Kelvin said. "I'm just not sure about the rental market around Martine, since it's not very near town. Most people who live out of town tend to own their own houses. Of course, there is the tourist market, but that's a whole different kettle of fish. Anyway, I'll work it out."

He laughed. "That's enough about me. I'm curious how you guys know about Martine, and why you want to go there specifically."

Kat and Blaine were both silent for a moment, both of them clearly wondering whether to tell him the truth.

Kat sighed. "We're looking for someone," she finally said. "We are doing research, and I am a writer, but the two things are not quite as connected as we led you to believe yesterday."

"I see," Kelvin said evenly. "Well, you'd just met me. I wouldn't expect you to spill your life story to me. You don't have to tell me any more if you don't want to. I'm not here to find out your business. I'm here to give you a ride."

"No, it's okay," Kat said. She asked him if he'd heard about the news story with the pig.

"Of course," he said.

"We're not sure if the man in that news story is who he says he is," Kat said. "We think he might be my friend's husband. He apparently faked his own death and came here to the Caribbean."

"Ah," Kelvin said. "I've heard that story before. The Caribbean seems to attract some unscrupulous characters, shady investors, money launderers, and the like. The authorities have been tightening up the regulations and the checks people go through to try to crack down on it, but Caribbean people are very freedom-loving. We don't want the government interfering in our every move."

"I understand," Blaine said. "Parts of the U.S. are like that, too."

Kelvin nodded. "Unfortunately, a few people see our lifestyle here in the Caribbean as an opportunity to take advantage of us."

They continued to talk, and soon arrived in Martine. Sammy woke up about halfway through the ride, and sat quite happily next to Kat as she stroked his head. He looked up at her lovingly.

The whole way, Kat had been wondering how they'd find the right house. But that went out of her mind very quickly, because as soon as they arrived in Martine, they saw a large crowd of people and numerous police cars parked in front of a house.

CHAPTER SEVENTEEN

Kelvin peered through the windshield as he drove. "What's this?" he said, looking out at the crowd of people blocking the street. They swarmed around the police cars, and there was a lot of shouting and talking.

"I have no idea," Kat said.

Kelvin could only drive a little way down the street, because it was jammed with people and vehicles, so he pulled over to the side of the street, parking with two wheels on the grassy edge next to it, two wheels on the street.

"Let's find out what's going on," Kelvin said. "Come on, Sammy, boy." He took a leash out of the driver's door and walked around to the back of the car to let Sammy out. He then clipped the leash on Sammy's collar.

Blaine and Kat got out and studied the crowd while they were waiting for Kelvin. "I think this is connected," Blaine said. "I just hope…"

"That the same people who left the pig for Richard and his girlfriend didn't come back and finish them off the same way they did the pig?" Kat said. "Yeah. I thought of that, too."

They started to walk down the shallow hill towards the crowd, following Kelvin and Sammy. Since they were the only nonlocal people there, most of the people who saw them did a little double-take, curious about why outsiders were present.

"Now this is what you call small town living," Kat said to Blaine under her breath.

"I'll say," Blaine agreed. "This looks like the sort of place where everyone has known everyone since the day they were born."

Kelvin overheard them. "It is that sort of place, although with more outsiders coming in, it's changing now. It used to be the kind of place where you could leave your front door wide open all day and go into town, come back, and everything would be in its place.

"In fact, you might even find some fresh potatoes or bananas or mangos or whatever on your kitchen table that a friendly neighbor had brought you."

"Sounds idyllic," Kat said.

"Yes, the old country life in Dominica was idyllic. When I was a little boy that way of life was still going on. But unfortunately, the more modern things have gotten, the less safe and happy it is. We didn't even have electricity growing up. Most people did, but not my family, as we were particularly poor, but that didn't stop us from enjoying ourselves.

"We'd stay up late into the night playing cards by oil lamp, having a marvelous time. And there was no TV for us, either, but us children didn't mind. We'd go out and play for hours and hours on end, catching land crabs in the gutters and swimming in the river and climbing trees. Those were the days."

Kat loved how it all sounded, and it got her creative writer's imagination going. But there was no more time to talk about that, since they'd reached the thick of the action.

"Follow me," Kelvin said, leading Kat and Blaine through the crowd, Sammy by his side. He walked up to one of the police, a woman standing by a patrol car.

"Good afternoon, ma'am," he said. "This is the house of the Americans?" *Looks like Kelvin was thinking the same thing Blaine and I were,* Kat thought, looking at Blaine meaningfully.

"Yes," she said, her eyes scanning quickly over him, the dog, Kat and Blaine. "Why? Can I help you?"

Kelvin gave a quick look back to Kat and Blaine as if to say 'trust me.' "I'm a tour guide, and these are my clients. They're friends of the couple who live here, and we just came to visit. Then we arrive to find this scene."

"Okay," the policewoman said, turning to Kat and Blaine. "I am very sorry, but I cannot tell you what has happened to your friends, because we don't know. Your friends are missing."

"Oh no," Kat said.

"Since when?" Blaine asked.

"We are not certain at present," the policewoman said. "There were reports of gunshots here this morning. When we got to the scene, the individuals were not here."

Kelvin looked towards the house, which was cordoned off with police tape. He frowned. "What evidence are you trying to conserve with the tape? Gunshot holes through the building?"

"Yes," the policewoman said. She eyed Kat and Blaine warily. "And blood... not much. Not consistent with them having been murdered here and the bodies moved. It is a relatively small amount. The pool of blood is no wider than six or eight inches."

Kat's mind was ticking. What on earth was going on? Some blood on the floor, gunshot damage to the house, and Richard and his woman friend missing?

"You definitely don't think they're dead?" Kat asked.

"We're treating this as a missing persons case rather than a murder investigation, yes," the policewoman said. A colleague came over to her and spoke in her ear. "I have to attend to something." Then she left.

Kelvin looked back at Kat and Blaine. "Well…" He puffed out a stream of air. "I suppose that's a little more drama than you bargained for."

"Yes, it's a complete surprise," Kat said. "I'm sorry you got dragged into all of this."

"No, it's fine," he said. "I think we should get closer to the house and see if the cops around it can give us any clues. They might have more information."

"Good idea," Blaine agreed.

They made their way through the crowd and soon arrived at the front by the house. With the tape around it, it really looked ominous.

"Hey, look," Kat said to Blaine and Kelvin, pointing to a bloody footprint on the veranda.

It was then that Sammy started to go wild. He barked, jumped up, and strained on the leash, so strongly that Kelvin, who was not a weak man, struggled to contain him. The dog was obviously desperate to go bounding up to the crime scene.

Kat looked at Blaine. "Do you think…?"

Kelvin nodded. "He smells the blood."

Blaine looked pale. "Maybe we should let him lead the way. Perhaps he could bring us to…"

Kat knew what words were coming next, even though he didn't say them: the bodies.

"Okay," Kelvin said. "Go on, Sammy. We're following you." He still held the leash tight, but followed in the direction Sammy wanted to go.

Sammy bounded forward up towards the house.

"Hey!" a police officer yelled at them. "No one can go near the crime scene. Get back!"

"Sorry, officer," Kelvin said, putting his hand up. He pulled Sammy back and off to the side, a little ways further off from the street than they were before.

Sammy began sniffing the ground manically, following his nose in a circle one way, then the other.

"He's onto something, isn't he?" Blaine said.

"I think so," Kat whispered. She was dreading what they were going to find.

Then Sammy started moving away from the street, pulling Kelvin after him, down a hill, and going in the direction of the nearby forest. Kelvin turned to Kat and Blaine, who were following him, and said with a grimace, "I think he knows exactly where he's going. We'd better brace ourselves."

"You don't have to do this," Kat said. "I'm sorry we got you involved in this."

"Looks like I'm in the thick of it already," Kelvin replied. "Let's keep going."

Blaine reached out and squeezed Kat's hand to give her some encouragement.

"Let's do this," Kat said.

They followed Sammy, and with his nose to the ground, he led them all the way down the hill and across a shallow ravine. The water was little more than a trickle, but Kat was glad she'd worn sneakers. After they crossed the ravine, there was a huge stretch of forest. Sammy was showing no signs of stopping, pulling Kelvin on through the trees.

"Oh boy," Kelvin said. "I've got a bad feeling about this."

"Tell me about it," Kat said. She was imagining Richard and his lover in the forest, dead.

How would Marion feel about that? To have found out her husband was alive, then to know he'd faked his own death to run off with another woman, and then to find out he'd been murdered? What a chaotic mix of intense, confusing emotions that was bound to bring about.

They traveled a good way into the forest, taking a left, then a right, then a left, twisting and turning through the trees, until they'd walked for about ten minutes. Kat was wondering how on earth they were going to find their way back.

All of a sudden, Kelvin held his arm up signaling for them to stop, then he turned and put his finger to his lips, indicating they should be quiet. He pointed between a gap in the trees.

Blaine and Kat both looked, but couldn't see anything at all except one tree after another.

Kelvin pointed again, and then Kat saw it. She gasped internally, but didn't do so out loud. They were very well concealed by bushes, and she didn't want to give away their whereabouts.

They could see a man, quite a ways away, leaning against a tree. He was talking to someone, because they could hear the buzz of two different voices, though they were too far away to make out their exact words. The other voice sounded masculine, as well. Kat didn't think the man was Richard, but the figure, although it was far away, was recognizable as a white man, so she couldn't rule it out.

"Stay here," Kelvin whispered to them. "I'm going to try to creep up on them."

"No," Blaine said. "It's too dangerous. We'll all go together."

"No," Kelvin countered. "They'll hear the sound of our feet. And look." He pulled up his shirt to reveal a gun. "It's a licenced firearm." He pulled it out. "Don't worry."

Kat felt terribly guilty. Kelvin was here in the forest on their account, and about to put himself in danger. Then again, he seemed willing, and perhaps even enjoying the adventure a little.

Blaine nodded. "Okay."

Kelvin began to inch forward with Sammy, as quietly as possible. Kat and Blaine hung back, watching him through the bushes. Kat said a silent prayer to herself, crossed her fingers, wished him all the luck in the world, and hoped they weren't all in terrible danger.

Kelvin was gaining on the two men, his gun held out in front of him, ready to shoot at any moment.

But then, just at the crucial moment, Sammy started barking.

CHAPTER EIGHTEEN

Kat's heart jumped up in her throat as she froze to the spot where she was standing.

Sammy's bark was loud and it echoed through the forest like a jet plane warming up to take off.

Kelvin and Sammy hadn't gone straight towards the men, because it would have made them too easy to spot. Rather, they'd gone around to the side, to make them less visible to the men.

"Is someone there?" one of the men hollered.

They all froze where they were except for Sammy, who continued to bark. Kelvin hung onto his leash grimly, grimacing as he gripped his gun.

"Let's go," one of the men said. "We need to get out of here."

All of a sudden there was the noise of the two men rushing through the bush, stepping on leaves and sticks.

"Hurry up!" one of the men said roughly.

"I'm trying," the other man yelled. "It's not easy with a bullet in my leg."

The voices were getting closer.

"Get over there," Blaine said to Kat, pointing to a nearby tree. "Hide behind it. They're coming our way."

"No," Kat said. "If we're going down, we're going down together. I say we come out and surprise them."

"No."

"Yes. We're doing it. Instinct, Blaine."

The voices of the men arguing were getting closer.

Kat jumped out from behind the bushes and shouted, "STOP WHERE YOU ARE!"

Both men jumped back, and one of them yelled with surprise. But the other man raised a gun and aimed it at Kat's head. "Who in the heck are you?"

"I'm not a cop," Kat said.

Blaine stepped out beside her. "She's not," he said

The other man drew his gun, too. "I don't care who they are. Let's blast them."

"No," Kelvin said, coming out from behind them, pointing his gun at them. "I only have one gun, but I have another weapon right here." He nodded at Sammy. "He will tear your throat out with one simple command."

One of the men, a tall man, laughed and said, "And a bullet will tear his out."

Kat realized she needed to break the standoff. "We're looking for Richard Molesey. Do you know where he is?"

The men looked at each other with surprise showing on their faces. "Who are you?" the shorter man, who was bleeding from his leg, asked.

Something suddenly clicked in Kat's mind. "You're the men who were in Marion Molesey's home, looking for Richard, aren't you?"

They looked at each other again, shocked.

"Small world, huh?" Blaine said grimly.

"Do you know where he is?" Kat repeated.

"He's gone," the taller man said. "He ran."

"You were here to kill him, I presume?" Kat asked evenly.

"If you go to the police, we will slit your throats," the smaller man said.

"Keep on and you better be prepared for this dog to maul you to death," Kelvin said.

The taller man, who was the more intimidating of the two, whirled around to face him. He pointed the gun at Sammy. "Not if I shoot him first."

For some reason that made Kat even more incensed than when they had their guns trained on her. "Coward," she screamed. "You're both cowards."

"You know..." the taller man began to say threateningly.

But the shorter man cried out in pain, clutching his leg.

"You need to get to a hospital," Kat said. "Who shot you? Was it Richard? You went in to kill Richard, but did he have a gun and shoot you?"

"Get out of here," the taller man said. "Get out, all three of you. And if you breathe a word to the police…"

"You'll slit my throat, yes," Kat said.

"We'll leave," Blaine said.

"Yes," Kelvin said. "Let's go."

"One thing," Kat interjected. "Why do you want to find Richard Molesey and kill him?"

"Let's just say he was caught up in one too many shady business deals," the taller man said. "And he crossed the wrong people."

"How did you know he was here?" Kat asked.

"You like to ask a lot of questions," the tall man said, a nasty glint in his eye. "Don't you know that curiosity killed the cat?"

"We're out of here," Kelvin said. Turning to Kat and Richard he continued, "The two of you walk ahead, and I'm going to walk behind you backwards, my gun on these two, before they try to shoot us in the back."

The taller man sneered, but the shorter man was in too much pain to be intimidating. Kat looked at him worriedly. "You might die if you don't get to hospital."

"Let him die," Kelvin said. "Let's go."

They started walking as Kelvin instructed, with Blaine and Kat up front, while he took up the rear, his gun still pointed at the two men, Sammy snarling all the way.

When they got far enough away and they couldn't see the men anymore, Kat breathed a sigh of relief. "Well, that was interesting."

"Do you think we should tell the police?" Kelvin asked.

"No," Kat said. "Maybe as we're leaving. Once we've found Richard Molesey, and we're out of here, then we can give the police the tip. Until then, I don't want to get tangled up in it. Next thing you know, we'll be charged with something."

"Sounds like a good idea," Blaine said. "We can even report it when we get back to Kansas."

"Agreed," Kat said.

"And I'll be back on St. Lucia," Kelvin said. "I didn't think you'd say that. I thought you'd want to go immediately to police. I'm glad you didn't go that route. I could do without the hassle. I have to get back to my job in a couple of days."

"We could do without the hassle, too," Kat said. "And the only person they pose a danger to is Richard Molesey. Hopefully, we'll have found him before we leave."

"Kelvin, we must insist you don't continue on with us," Blaine said. "You've put yourself in far too much danger on our account already. You've gone above and beyond."

"Thanks, and I was happy to do it," Kelvin said. "But I have to agree with you. I'll take you back to your hotel, however beyond that, I'm afraid I'll have to duck out. I have some family to visit and want to spend some more time with my daughter before I go back to St. Lucia."

"Good," Kat said. "I was worried you'd insist on accompanying us." She grinned. "Thankfully you're much more sensible than that." She bent down and patted Sammy. "Thank you, too, big boy. You were a great help."

They soon came to the edge of the forest. Kelvin frowned. "I think we should find another way to get out of here and avoid the crowd before the police start asking us questions."

"Good idea," Blaine said. He looked around. "Do you think we can go along the edge of the forest here, and then go up that hill over there," Blaine said as he pointed in the direction of a nearby hill.

"Yes, that's just what I was thinking," Kelvin said. "I think that'll take us back to the main road. We'll have just a short walk back to the car."

They followed the route, and thankfully, it worked. Kat and Blaine decided they needed to rent a car, so Kelvin took them to a rental car company in Roseau. The whole drive back, he was silent, putting on some loud Calypso music, making it clear he didn't want to talk.

Kat caught sight of his eyes in the rearview mirror, and he looked exhausted. She didn't blame him. She felt very grateful for all the help he'd given them, and told him so when they were getting out of his car at the rental car company.

"It's nothing," he said.

"I wish there was something we could do to repay you," Blaine said.

"Not at all, not at all," Kelvin replied. "Don't worry at all."

"I hope it hasn't put you off buying property in the area," Blaine said.

Kelvin grinned. "I don't scare that easily."

"Say goodbye to Sammy for us," Kat said as she looked in the back seat of the car where the big dog was sleeping.

"I will."

And with that, he was gone.

Kat and Blaine turned to each other, and breathed a huge sigh of relief.

"Well," Blaine said. "That was something."

"Wasn't it just?" Kat said. "But we have a little time to process it now. If we got into Richard's email that easily, those men who were at Marion's probably did too and figured out Richard was here because of the airline tickets. It looks like Richard shot that short man when they came to kill him, and then ran. My guess is Richard and the woman will be trying to get out of the country."

"I agree."

"But probably not on a plane. I'm thinking if there's a missing persons flag on Richard and his girlfriend, they won't try to leave by any channels where they'd have to show their passports. Who knows? Maybe they didn't even have enough time to grab their passports before they left."

"You're right, which means they wouldn't be leaving on a commercial airline flight."

"Unless it's a private plane," Kat mused. "Or…"

"A private boat," Blaine said.

"You read my mind. I was thinking a yacht." Kat's brain was working overtime. "We need to rent a car and get to the marina.

"Let's do it," Blaine said.

CHAPTER NINETEEN

Kat and Blaine easily rented a car. The rental agency was very busy, and the only car it could give them was a small hatchback, which they weren't used to. But it did the job of getting them to the marina as quickly as possible.

They were disheartened to discover from the car rental agent that the marina was about a forty-minute drive from where they were, on the other side of the island.

"No use complaining about it," Blaine said. "All we can do is get there as fast as we can."

"You take the wheel," Kat said. "You're better at driving fast." She raised her eyebrow, since she'd often told him he was driving too fast when they were in Kansas.

"See?" he said triumphantly, getting into the front seat. "My love of speed is finally paying off."

"Okay, Mario Andretti," Kat said with a laugh. "Pedal to the metal."

"Yes, ma'am." Blaine pulled out of the rental car parking lot and quickly got out onto the highway. "This car may be small, but she has quite a little kick."

"Thank goodness," Kat said. "I was worried it wouldn't be able to get beyond sixty miles an hour."

"No troubles there," Blaine said.

The scenery on the way to the marina was absolutely beautiful, as the highway curved around the coast, giving them wonderful views out to sea. It was a clear day, with perfect cotton candy clouds floating across the sky. But there was little time to admire the view. Kat's mind was racing at a million miles an hour, wondering where they could look for Richard and his girlfriend if there was no sign of them at the marina.

But as it turned out, that wasn't a problem.

They drove into the marina parking lot, which was surrounded by a bank and numerous restaurants and bars. It would have been a nice place to spend a little time, Kat thought, if they'd been on vacation. She allowed an image to flash through her mind, an image of Blaine and her having a victory drink while they overlooked the moored yachts and boats bobbing up and down on the gentle waves.

"Let's go over to that booth," Kat said as Blaine parked the car. She pointed to a security booth at the entry to the marina walkway. "They might have seen something."

"Good idea."

They quickly left the car and ran over to the booth. There was a uniformed woman inside who looked bored, playing on her phone. Kat supposed there wasn't much for her to do in the booth.

"Good morning," Kat said, checking her watch as an afterthought. It was close to noon. "We're looking for some people. A white man and woman. Did they come here and take a boat out?"

She looked at them blankly. "I'm not sure, sorry."

Probably looking down at her phone at the time, Kat thought.

"Okay," Kat said. "Never mind."

"You could ask him," the woman said, pointing to another booth at the other end of the marina. It had been hidden from their view because it was blocked by a row of restaurants when they were in the parking lot.

"Thank you, we will," Blaine said.

They hurried over to it, but had a similarly disappointing response.

"Sorry," the man said. "I came on my shift about an hour ago. I haven't seen any white couple go out on a boat, but they might have done it before I got here."

"Well, thank you, anyway," Kat said.

Kat and Blaine walked away and hovered by the water's edge, wondering what to do next.

"We could check the airport," Blaine said. "See if your private plane idea was right."

"Hmm," Kat said, unconvinced. "I don't know. My gut is telling me not to leave here yet."

"Okay," Blaine said. "Well, you're the seasoned investigator, so I'm going to follow your lead."

"That's the thing…" Kat said. "I don't know what to do. I think I need to clear my head. Let's go get a drink and sit down and relax. Maybe then I'll be able to think of something."

"All right. That's a good idea."

They went into a nearby bar. Blaine got a cold beer and Kat, after a long look at the cocktail list, selected a glass of white wine. She was beginning to get hungry, but ordering food felt too much like a waste of time, like giving up, so she didn't. Blaine didn't seem to feel the same and got a tuna sandwich.

They sat outside, overlooking the water.

A cheerful-looking man came striding toward the bar area on the marina walkway, obviously having just come off a boat. He had quite a presence, very tall and slim, with an energetic way of walking.

Blaine nodded towards him to Kat. "He's got a lot of energy."

"He certainly has."

The man caught them looking at him and waved. He said something with a smile to the woman in the security booth, and walked over to Kat and Blaine.

"Morning," he said with a friendly manner. "I saw you were looking at me."

"We were admiring your energy and flair," Kat said.

He laughed. "Thanks, man. I'm Lucius." He shook both their hands.

Kat and Blaine introduced themselves.

"Great to meet you," he said. "Now, tell me, would you like a ride on my speedboat? You look like my kind of people. Relaxed and taking y'all time."

Kat and Blaine shared a slightly amused look, given they were pretty far from relaxed and taking their time at the moment.

"Do you work here?" Kat asked. "Were you here this morning?"

"I've been in and out, in and out," he said. "Why do you ask?"

"We're looking for a white couple, a man and a woman."

He gestured at the two of them. "You don't need to look very far," he said, laughing.

"No, someone else. They may have come here and gotten a boat. We're not sure, but…"

"There were three white couples here this morning that went out."

Kat looked at Blaine, her heart rate rising. "Really?" she asked Lucius.

He nodded.

"Two of them keep their yachts here. We get a lot of island hoppers. I know some of them, they come around every couple of years…"

"And the other couple?" Blaine asked.

"I'd never seen them before," Lucius said. "They hired a yacht and took off. Seemed to be in a hurry."

Kat got up from her seat. "Was the guy quite tall, with brown hair, and she was short and blonde?"

"Yes," Lucius said.

"How long ago was it? Can we go after them?"

"About two hours ago," Lucius said. "Might be a bit of a job to find them, but it can be done. Could take some time…"

He was clearly hinting about payment.

"Whatever it takes," Blaine said. "However long."

"It's forty U.S. dollars an hour," Lucius said.

"Fine," Kat said. "Let's go, and let's go now."

"Not going to finish your drinks?" Lucius asked.

"No," Kat said. "Now is not the time to be leisurely. We've got to find them, and we've got to find them fast."

Lucius looked at her with a worried look on his face. "You're not dragging me into some drug cartel war, are you?"

"No," Kat said, as they took off toward the marina walkway and the speedboat. "We're looking for a missing person. Well, he changed his identity and came out here, leaving a wife and four children at home, one of whom is very sick."

"Selfish brute," Lucius said, and called Richard a curse word.

"To say the least," Blaine said. "I can't stand a man who runs away from his responsibilities."

"He's not a man, he's a little boy who never grew up," Lucius said. "I have three children, and I wouldn't want to be away from them longer than a week or so. They need me."

"Yes, I agree." Kat said.

They were walking fast and very soon they were at Lucien's speedboat.

"Let me fire this baby up," Lucius said as they climbed in.

"What's her name?" Blaine asked.

Lucius grinned. "Speed Demon."

"Sounds good to me," Kat said.

"The two of you can swim, right?"

"Yes," Blaine said.

"Good, but I still want you to put on these life preservers. Just in case." He started the engine, pushed the throttle, and they were off. They quickly gained speed.

Kat kept her eyes on the horizon for any sign of boats.

Lucius looked back and saw what she was doing. "I think it'll be a half hour or so before we'll be able to see them, but keep an eye out anyway. They may not have gone far. Thankfully it's a clear day."

An agonizingly long twenty minutes passed.

But finally, Lucius, whose eyesight was very acute said, "Look! Two yachts!"

Kat looked into the distance and could just about make them out. "Your vision is a lot better than mine."

"It comes from experience," Lucius said. "I've been out on boats for thirty years. Probably more."

The yachts were far away from each other, clearly not traveling together.

"The question is," Blaine said, voicing what they were all thinking, "which one to go after?"

"We'll just have to pick one," Lucius said, "then if we're wrong, we'll try the other one."

"Yes," Kat said. "And also keep in mind that neither of them may be the right boat."

"We'll get there in the end," Lucius said confidently. "Now, tell me, which boat do you want to go for? I've got great faith in women's intuition."

Kat looked at both of them. She thought about where they might be going, and which one might be more likely to have Richard and his girlfriend on board. There was no way to tell, and her brain was tying itself up in knots.

"Don't think too much about it," Lucius said after she'd been quiet for a while. "Just go with your gut instinct."

"Okay," Kat said. She took a deep breath, and pointed to the one on the left. "That one."

"I'm on it," Lucius exclaimed. Kat thought the speedboat was already going as fast as it could, but Lucius kicked it up even more, and soon they were zooming through the water at lightning speed.

They were going so fast Kat had to grip onto the side of the boat, afraid she might fall out. Although she was a strong swimmer, she didn't want to test her skills if she fell out going at such a high rate of speed.

Lucius gained on the yacht, and soon they were close enough to make out two figures, a man and a woman.

"It could be them!" Blaine said.

As they drew closer, Kat's hopes were confirmed and her instincts had been right. It was Richard and his girlfriend.

CHAPTER TWENTY

Lucius brought the speedboat up to the rear of the yacht, then moved slightly to the left so he could drive up alongside it.

"Can we just... jump on their boat? You know, like you see on TV," Kat asked.

"Yes," Lucius said. "Yachts move far slower than the type of boat I have, so when I get closer, I'll slow down, and you can jump onboard the yacht."

Kat took a deep breath. "Okay."

Blaine squeezed her hand. "Don't worry. We can do this."

As they got closer to the yacht, they saw Richard and his girlfriend watching them, looking very worried.

Lucius expertly pulled the speedboat up next to the yacht. Kat and Blaine held hands and jumped from the speedboat onto the yacht.

Richard's gun was aimed at them as soon as they were on the boat. "Who are you, and what are you doing here?" His girlfriend cowered behind him.

"You're Richard Moseley, aren't you?" Kat asked in an accusing tone of voice.

He looked shocked. "No, no, I have no idea who that is. I'm Michael Tomlinson."

"Give it up, Richard," Blaine said. "We're from Lindsay, and we know all about you."

"Yes," Kat said. "All about your wife Marion, and your teenaged kids. And your daughter, Betsy, who is so, so sick. And you, who let them grieve for you while you're here living the life of Riley in the Caribbean. Or at least trying to."

"One of your kids is sick? And they're teenagers? You told me they were adults," the girlfriend said.

"You have no room to talk, Helen. You have two small kids of your own that you left," he said as he turned towards her, bringing the gun down.

"The name's Rebecca," she yelled at him. "Remember?"

Kat took the opportunity of the gun being diverted away from her and charged at him with her full force. He fell to the deck, the gun flying out of his hand and landing in front of Kat. She lost her footing for a moment, but was able to grab the gun off the deck. Blaine pulled her back and got her as far away from Richard as was possible.

"Nice move, lady!" Lucius called appreciatively from the speedboat.

"I'm not going to use this on you," Kat said to Richard and Rebecca, or Helen, whatever her name was. "I'm just making sure you don't use it on us."

"Give that back to me," Richard said, snarling.

Kat was suddenly consumed with so much rage for what he'd

done to Marion and their poor children, that she threw the gun over the side of the yacht.

"What did you do that for, you stupid woman?" Richard raged, looking over the side as the gun sank in the ocean.

Kat, anger pumping through her body, said, "Aren't you ashamed of yourself for what you've done to Marion and your children?"

"You don't know what you're talking about," Richard spat. "People were trying to kill me. I had to get away."

"They still are!" Kat said. "That's why you're here on this boat, isn't it? You're trying to run away from them. You didn't think they'd come all the way from the U.S. to track you down, but they did. Then you shot one of them in the leg and ran away."

Richard frowned. "How do you know all this stuff? Who are you?"

"I'm Kat Denham," she said. "I met Marion at the tennis club in Lindsay. She sent me to find you."

"How did she know I wasn't dead?" he asked.

"Someone left a note for her at your home after your funeral, telling her to look further into it," Kat said.

"But how did you know we were here?" the woman said, tears welling up in her eyes.

"So now you're going to cry," Kat said angrily to Helen, "because your fake little perfect life is ruined? Maybe Richard should have thought about how his kids would feel about his death, and maybe you should have thought of yours, too."

Kat took a deep breath, feeling her hands shaking with rage. "We found you because Richard bought tickets to St. Lucia using his home computer and email. Serious rookie mistake, Richard. I imagine that's how those men tracked you down, too. Your email was pretty easy to hack into."

The woman hit Richard on the arm, hard. "How could you be so stupid?" she screamed.

Richard was in tears himself now. He looked at Blaine, "Don't look so high and mighty. If you'd been in my shoes, you'd have done the same thing."

"Never in a billion years," Blaine said. "I believe in my responsibility to my family."

"So do I!" he said. "That's why I had to get out. I'd cut a shady business deal, I won't lie, but that was only to get the money we needed to pay Betsy's medical bills."

"You said it was the cash we needed to start our new life," the woman said.

"No, it wasn't," he said desperately. "Then it got dangerous, so I knew I had to get out of there and fake my own death to keep my family from harm."

"Yeah, sure," Kat said. "Anyway, it didn't keep them from harm, because those two men turned up at Marion's home and tied the kids up."

"They did?" Richard said, clearly shocked.

"You would have known, if you'd been there to protect them," Blaine said, sounding as angry as Kat.

"And if the money was for Betsy..." Kat began.

"It wasn't," the woman sobbed. "Richard, you told me it was for us and our beautiful new life. Isn't that right?"

Kat and Blaine looked at each other in disbelief. This woman wanted their love affair to be more important than the medical needs of his sick child? The whole thing was mind-boggling.

"Well, I must say, you're well matched," Kat said. "You're both as selfish and despicable as the other. I hope you find a desert island somewhere to live out the rest of your selfish lives without affecting other people. How did the two of you meet?" Kat asked.

The woman wrapped her arm around Richard. "We met on one of his business trips to New York. We fell so in love, and both found family life to be ever so boring, so we decided to get fake passports, and..."

"Shut up!" Richard yelled at her. "Just shut up!"

"What a mess," Kat said, shaking her head. "If there was a Hall of Fame for bad decision-making, Richard, I think you'd be in the number one spot."

Richard sat down and held his head in his hands. "I think you're right. Seeing you, from Lindsay, here now... It brings it all back to reality. I thought I could escape and live in a dream world."

"Don't even think about it," the woman yelled. "You're not leaving me!"

"Richard, you need to do the following things," Kat said to him. "Transfer the largest sum of money you possibly can to Marion's account. We can do that right now." She took out her phone. "You can log into your online banking on this. Then you need to apologize to Marion. After that go back to the United States and turn yourself in for fraud."

The woman was crying and so dramatic, Kat could barely hear herself think.

"Will you just be quiet for a moment?" Kat said. But the woman didn't even hear Kat.

"All right," Richard said. "I'll do all those things. I will. I'll face up to my responsibilities, and do whatever's necessary for my family."

"Good man," Blaine said.

But suddenly, without warning, Richard jumped up, and stormed across the yacht. He launched himself into the speedboat, pushed Lucius off the boat, pulled the throttle back, and with a roar of the powerful engine, he was gone.

"Richard!" the woman cried out after him, but he never looked back.

"Lucius!" Kat and Blaine yelled, looking over the side and into the water. They couldn't see him anywhere.

A few moments later as Kat and Blaine frantically searched for him, Lucius appeared at the rear of the yacht, dripping wet as he pulled himself up and over the transom.

"I'm sorry," he said, panting. "I should have stopped him. I wasn't looking when he shoved me over the side of my boat."

"No, no, don't blame yourself. It's not your fault," Kat said, watching Richard speed away into the distance.

Lucius walked over to them and shook his head. "What a piece of work that man is."

Kat felt like bursting into tears. "I've let him get away. I've failed Marion, and now she and the children won't get their money."

Blaine put his arms around her and hugged her. "Don't say that. For one, you found him. You went to so much effort to find him. You've done Marion proud. Secondly, we can call the Coast Guard and let them know what's going on."

"Yes, that needs to be done." Lucius said. "I have their number. I'll call now."

He called the Coast Guard and then sailed the yacht back to the marina. Lucius had been right. The yacht was very slow, so it was a long ride. Kat was full of mixed emotions, and having Rebecca/Helen continuously wailing and crying wasn't helping.

After she'd listened to her for a while, Kat began to feel a little sorry for her. All of her hopes and dreams had come crashing down around her. Her new life had fallen completely apart in a matter of just a few minutes.

But then Kat remembered that this woman had children of her own that she'd left, small children, and all Kat's empathic feelings towards her vanished. How must the children have felt? Where were they? Who were they with? Did they think she'd died?

This woman had clearly expected that she and Richard would ride off into the sunset and live happily ever after, as if their old lives had never existed. But what she hadn't realized was there was only one person at the center of Richard's life, and that was Richard.

When they got back to the marina, there were a number of things they had to do. Talk with the Coast Guard, tell the police what had happened, call the police in the U.S., and arrange to get back to St. Lucia. They decided they wouldn't stay in the Caribbean and wait until Richard was caught. With a good lawyer it could take months to resolve his case, after he was arrested.

Besides, Kat had found out the truth. What she knew now would at least be enough to give Marion closure.

The more she thought about Marion and her children, the worse she felt for them. It would have been much easier for them to believe he'd died. At least then they could have believed he'd been a good man who'd put them first, but had died to a freak accident.

As it was, they had to come to terms with the reality of a man, who, under the veneer of acting like a caring family man, was cruel, careless, and ultimately, completely selfish.

She felt sick as the yacht slowly sailed back inside the protected harbour of the marina. She turned to Lucius. "I'm so sorry," she said. "We never should have asked you to find the yacht, and now your boat is gone."

"We'll transfer the money for you to get a new boat. In fact, we'll do it now." She saw Blaine shake his head in agreement.

"I couldn't ask you to do that," Lucius said. "It was not your fault. I don't have insurance, but I'll make it…"

"No," Blaine said. "The loss of your boat is entirely our fault and our responsibility." He folded up two U.S. $100-dollar bills and handed them to him. "And here's the money for the boat ride."

"Why don't we sit down, have a drink. and calm our nerves," Kat said. "Then we can do the banking online and get it transferred to you."

"If you insist," Lucius said.

Kat found a smile from somewhere, and said decisively, "I do."

EPILOGUE

The tennis club was having a barbecue. It was the end of spring and a perfect time for it.

Marion Molesey had become an entirely different woman. She'd had her hair highlighted and cut into a long-layered style that framed her face. She wore brighter colors now, but that wasn't where the real change had taken place. That was only the surface, the frosting on the cake, so to speak.

The deep and meaningful change came from within her. She didn't look tortured anymore. She didn't bite her nails. Her eyes shone with happiness. And most importantly, she was free.

Kat had been surprised when she'd returned from Dominica and St. Lucia with the news about her husband. She'd been worried Marion would have a breakdown when she found out about Richard, and she'd asked Lennon and Mitzi to help her, just in case.

But Marion didn't get sad. She got angry. And that anger stoked a fire in her, a fire she used to change her life.

She was even more ferocious on the tennis court now than she'd been previously. She'd moved up the ranks, and she even started competing in advanced tournaments.

She stopped taking no for an answer with the doctors regarding Betsy's condition. She had numerous other tests done, got some new medication for Betsy's symptoms, and soon, although no one knew exactly what was going on with her health, Betsy began to feel much better. She even made it to the tennis club barbecue.

Marion had warmed up to the silver fox, who was actually a club member, and enjoyed puttering around the tennis club, helping with the plants. Instead of pushing away his advances and blushing and scurrying away when he'd asked her out, she'd held her head up high, smiled, and said, "Yes. I'd absolutely love to."

When the time had come to testify in court as a witness against Richard – he'd been hauled back to America and brought up on four charges – she didn't shed a single tear. Kat had gone along with her for support, but Marion had been so confident and fabulous, she didn't need any support. She looked like she owned the courtroom.

During the trial they found out who was responsible for the note telling Marion Richard's death could have been faked. It was one of the workers at the whitewater rafting center, who'd had some suspicions about the accident.

The two businessmen from Houston were arrested in Dominica, and were brought up on charges of attempted murder against Richard. They failed to post bail and were held for such a long time that the U.S. government got the Dominican government to agree to their extradition, so they could be tried for the incident in Marion's home where they'd tied up the children. They were convicted and were serving fifteen years each for that crime.

Marion was the life of the barbecue, laughing with her silver fox, and chatting with everyone and anyone she met. She said how much she was looking forward to playing tennis after the barbecue. They were having a tournament that evening, and everyone knew it was highly likely she'd win the women's division.

She was so in-demand that Kat could barely find a moment to speak with her. But later, Marion came up to Kat and said, "Do you have time for a little walk?"

"Sure," Kat said.

They walked down a flower-lined path alone.

"Kat, I wanted to say thank you again."

Kat smiled. "You're welcome, but you've already said it about a hundred times now."

Marion laughed. "I know. I was just wondering, well, the courts have granted me a divorce, and they've split the assets Richard and I owned, so I've come into a good deal of money. I never knew Richard had so much tucked away."

"That's fantastic," Kat said. "I'm so glad. That will make everything so much easier for you."

"Yes," Marion said. "Believe me, I'm glad, too. What I wanted to ask, Kat, is can I take you on a vacation? Lennon and Mitzi could come to, if you'd like. I just want to give you an amazing trip, where all you have to do is relax. No working. And strictly no investigating."

Kat grinned. "Wow! What a treat!"

"That's the idea, Kat. Where would you like to go? Europe? The Seychelles? Japan?"

"My goodness," Kat said. "I've never thought about it, but I must admit, the Seychelles sound lovely."

"The Seychelles it is then," Marion said, nodding decisively. "Unless you decide otherwise. We don't have to book it yet. Just start thinking about it."

"I will," Kat said. She gave Marion a hug. "Thank you so much."

"No, thank you," Marion said. "I'll never be able to repay you for what you did for me. It changed my life."

Kat felt something deep within her spirit move, though she wasn't sure what. Perhaps it was an "end of an era" feeling. She'd already promised Blaine she wouldn't investigate anymore. She was very much enjoying looking after Florence two days a week, working at improving her tennis game, writing her books, and spending more time with Jazz and Rudy.

She also volunteered with underprivileged children once a week, which she adored and gave her a sense of meaning and purpose.

Her new life was already well underway. But somehow, this vacation seemed like the perfect way to close the chapter on her investigating life.

"Marion, this means more than you'll ever know."

RECIPES

CREAMY GARLIC MUSHROOMS AND BACON

Ingredients:
4 bacon strips, fried in a cast iron skillet, crumbled
1 tbsp. unsalted butter
1 box whole brown mushrooms, bottom of stems removed
1/2 tbsp. olive oil
¼ cup dry white wine
4 cloves garlic, minced
¾ cups heavy cream
½ tsp. fresh thyme
Salt and freshly ground pepper to taste
¼ cup grated mozzarella
¼ cup shredded or grated parmesan cheese

Directions:
Preheat broiler. Fry bacon in cast iron skillet (or other oven safe skillet) until crispy. Remove bacon to a paper-lined plate and set aside. Pour out remaining bacon grease. In same pan, melt the butter, add mushrooms, drizzle with olive oil, and mix together, scraping up any browned bacon bits from the bottom of the pan.

Cook 2-3 minutes until lightly browned and mushrooms have released their juices. Add wine and reduce over medium heat for 2-3 minutes, stirring occasionally.

Add the garlic and stir to combine. Add cream and herbs, reduce heat to low and gently simmer until sauce is slightly thickened (about 4-5 minutes.) Season with salt and pepper. Crumble the bacon and add to the mix. Top the mushrooms with the mozzarella and parmesan cheese.

Place skillet under broiler and broil until the cheese is melted and bubbly, about 3-5 minutes.

Serves 2. Double ingredients for 4 servings. Enjoy!

SHELLEY'S CHEWY CHOCOLATE CHIP OATMEAL COOKIES

Ingredients:
1 cup unsalted butter, softened
1 cup light brown sugar, tightly packed
½ cup white sugar
2 eggs, extra large
2 tsp. vanilla extract (Don't use imitation.)
1 ¼ cups all-purpose flour
½ tsp. baking soda
1 tsp. salt
3 cups quick cooking oats
1 cup chopped walnuts (I like to use cashews.)
1 cup semisweet chocolate chips

Directions:
Preheat oven to 325 degrees. Butter or use parchment paper on baking sheets. In a large bowl, cream together the butter, brown sugar, and white sugar until smooth. Beat in the eggs, one at a time. Stir in vanilla.

Combine the flour, baking soda, and salt. Stir into the creamed mixture until just blended. Mix in the quick oats, walnuts, and chocolate chips. Drop heaping teaspoonfuls of cookie batter onto prepared baking sheets.

Bake for 12-14 minutes in the preheated oven. Allow cookies to cool on baking sheets before transferring to a wire rack to cool completely.

SPINACH FETA CALZONE CASSEROLE

Ingredients:

Dough:
1 pkg. dry yeast (about 2 ¼ tsp.)
¾ cup warm water (100 to 110)
1 tsp. olive oil
2 cups all-purpose flour
½ tsp. salt
Cooking spray

Filling:
3 tsp. olive oil, divided
5 garlic cloves, thinly sliced and divided
1 medium onion, thinly sliced
¼ tsp. salt
¼ tsp. crushed red pepper
2 lbs. coarsely chopped fresh spinach
¾ cup crumbled feta cheese

Directions:

Dough:
Dissolve yeast in warm water in a small bowl. Let stand 5 minutes. Stir in olive oil. Combine flour and salt in a large bowl. Add yeast mixture, stirring until dough forms. Turn dough out onto a lightly floured surface.

Knead until smooth and elastic (about 6 minutes). Place dough in a large bowl coated with cooking spray, turning to coat the top of it. Cover and let rise in a warm place for 1 ½ hours or until doubled in size.

Preheat oven to 425 degrees. Punch dough down. Cover and let rest 5 minutes. Roll dough into a 12" square. Fit dough into an 8" square baking pan coated with cooking spray, allowing excess dough to hang over edges of dish.

Filling:

Combine 1 tsp. olive oil and 2 garlic cloves. Set aside. Heat remaining 2 tsp. olive oil over medium-high heat. Add remaining garlic cloves and onion. Sauté until onion is lightly browned. Spoon mixture into a large bowl. Stir in salt and pepper.

Keep warm. Add half of spinach to pan. Cook 1 minute until spinach begins to wilt, stirring frequently. Add remaining spinach. Cook until spinach wilts. Place spinach in a colander and squeeze moisture out. Add spinach and cheese to onion mixture, stirring until well combined.

Brush dough with half of garlic-oil mixture. Top with spinach mixture. Fold excess dough over filling to cover. Brush with remaining garlic-oil mixture. Bake at 425 for 30 minutes until golden. Let stand 10 minutes. Serve and enjoy!

CHOCOLATE MOUSSE CHEESECAKE

Ingredients:

Crust:
1 ½ cups chocolate wafer crumbs (about 24 wafers)
1/3 cup finely chopped pecans (I like to use cashews.)
2 tbsp. sugar
1/3 cup unsalted butter, melted

Filling:
2 pkgs. (8 oz. each) cream cheese, room temperature
½ cup sugar
1 tsp. lemon juice

1 tsp. lemon peel, grated
1 tsp. vanilla extract (Don't use imitation.)
2 eggs, yolks and whites separated

Topping:
1 cup semisweet chocolate chips
5 tbsp. butter, cubed
4 egg yolks
¼ cup confectioners' sugar
2 tbsp. strong brewed coffee
1 tsp. vanilla extract
½ cup heavy whipping cream, whipped
Optional: ½ cup whipped cream for dollop on top

Directions:
Preheat oven to 375 degrees. In a small bowl combine the wafer crumbs, pecans, and sugar. Stir in butter until crumbly. Press onto the bottom and 1 ½" up the sides of a greased 9" springform pan. Place pan on baking sheet. Bake at 375 degrees for 8 minutes. Cool on a wire cooking rack. Reduce heat to 325 degrees.

Filling:
In a large bowl beat cream cheese and sugar until smooth. Beat in lemon juice, lemon peel, and vanilla. Add egg yolks. Beat on low speed until combined. In a small bowl beat egg whites on high until stiff peaks form. Fold in into cream cheese mixture. Pour into crust. Return pan to baking sheet. Bake for 25-30 minutes or until the center is almost set. Cool on a wire rack for 10 minutes.

Topping:
In a microwave, melt chocolate and butter. Stir until smooth. In a small heavy saucepan, whisk egg yolks, sugar, and coffee. Cook and stir over low heat until mixture reaches 160 degrees, about 5 minutes (may vary with your stove.) Stir in vanilla. Whisk in chocolate mixture. Set saucepan in ice and stir until cooled, about 2 minutes. Fold in whipped cream. Spread over cheesecake and refrigerate until set. Remove sides of pan. If desired, garnish with whipped cream. Serve and enjoy!

SAUSAGE PLAIT (PICNIC PIE)

Ingredients:
1 tbsp. olive oil
1 red onion, peeled and finely sliced
1 sprig fresh sage, leaves chopped
6 pork sausages
¼ cup breadcrumbs
¼ tsp. freshly grated nutmeg
8 oz. ready-made puff pastry
1 extra large egg
1 tbsp. milk

Directions:
Preheat oven to 350 degrees. Heat the olive oil in a fry pan over medium low heat and add the onion. Cook for 20 minutes or until soft and golden brown. Add the sage leaves, cook for 2 minutes. Remove from pan and spread on a plate to cool.

On a floured work surface, roll the pastry into a large rectangle, ¼" thick, and cut lengthwise into two long, even rectangles. Then cut each one into 3 pieces. Spread onion mixture on pastry. Place sausage on it. Wrap the sausage with the pastry.

Mix the egg and milk. Brush the pastry with the mixture, then fold one side of the pastry over, wrapping the filling inside. Press down with your fingers or the edge of a spoon to seal the seam.

Cut the rolls into about 2-3 inches and space them out on a cookie sheet, cut sausage side down. Brush the rolls with the rest of the egg wash and bake in preheated oven for 25 minutes or until, puffed, golden and cooked through. Serve and enjoy!

LEAVE A REVIEW

I'd really appreciate it you could take a few seconds and leave a review of Missing in the Islands.

Just go to the link below. Thank you so much, it means a lot to me ~ Dianne

http://getbook.at/MITI

Paperbacks & Ebooks for FREE

Go to www.dianneharman.com/freepaperback.html and get your FREE copies of Dianne's books and favorite recipes immediately by signing up for her newsletter.

Once you've signed up for her newsletter you're eligible to win three paperbacks. One lucky winner is picked every week. Hurry before the offer ends!

ABOUT THE AUTHOR

Dianne lives in Huntington Beach, California, with her husband, Tom, a former California State Senator, and her boxer dog, Kelly. Her passions are cooking, reading, and dogs, so whenever she has a little free time, you can either find her in the kitchen, playing with Kelly in the back yard, or curled up with the latest book she's reading. Her award-winning books include:

Cedar Bay Cozy Mystery Series

Cedar Bay Cozy Mystery Series - Boxed Set

Liz Lucas Cozy Mystery Series

Liz Lucas Cozy Mystery Series - Boxed Set

High Desert Cozy Mystery Series

High Desert Cozy Mystery Series - Boxed Set

Northwest Cozy Mystery Series

Northwest Cozy Mystery Series - Boxed Set

Midwest Cozy Mystery Series

Midwest Cozy Mystery Series - Boxed Set

Jack Trout Cozy Mystery Series

Cottonwood Springs Cozy Mystery Series

Cottonwood Springs Mystery Series – Boxed Set

Coyote Series

Midlife Journey Series

Red Zero Series, Black Dot Series

The Holly Lewis Mystery Series

Newsletter

If you would like to be notified of her latest releases please go to www.dianneharman.com and sign up for her newsletter.

Website: www.dianneharman.com,
Blog: www.dianneharman.com/blog
Email: dianne@dianneharman.com

PUBLISHING 11/15/19

DEATH IN THE BAY

BOOK SEVENTEEN OF

THE CEDAR BAY COZY MYSTERY SERIES

http://getbook.at/DITB

A man falls overboard and dies in the bay.

Was it an accident or a calculated murder motivated by a changed inheritance? Unfaithful spouses? Revenge?

When the dead man is Sheriff's Mike oldest friend and one of the heirs is his goddaughter, he has to find out what happened. Good thing he has Kelly and a big boxer to help him.

This is the 17th book in the Cedar Bay Cozy Mystery Series by a two-time USA Today Bestselling Author.

Open your smartphone, point and shoot at the QR code below. You will be taken to Amazon where you can pre-order 'Death in The Bay'.

(Download the QR code app onto your smartphone from the iTunes or Google Play store in order to read the QR code below.)

Made in the
USA
Middletown, DE